DARK SEAS

KARI LEE HARMON

PUBLISHER'S NOTE: This is a work of fiction. Names, characters, places, and incidents either are the product of the author's imagination or are used fictitiously. Any resemblance to actual persons, living or dead, business establishments, events or locales is entirely coincidental.

Copyright © Kari Lee Harmon

Published by Oliver Heber Books

THE SEAS WERE dark that day. Bob stared out of his tiny Boston apartment window at the ocean before him. He couldn't afford anything bigger, but at least he had a view of the sea. Whitecaps crested on the tops of massive rolling waves; their power fierce against those who dared brave her cold waters. Late spring in New England could be a bitch, but he welcomed her rage. He could relate. Thirty years with the Bureau, and this is what his life had come to: forced early retirement, a wife who had cheated on and then divorced him, and a son he'd let down, leaving Bob with nothing left but a lonely friend found deep inside a bottle.

He pressed his lips against the rim of the brown glass and sipped slowly, relishing the burn of the whiskey sliding down his throat to warm his insides. Funny thing. No matter how much he drank, he could never seem to chase away the chill and the thought of food turned his stomach. He glanced at the stale, cold, untouched pizza on his kitchen table but didn't remember ordering it. His brow knit together in concentration, but the ever-present fog lingered in his brain. He felt cold and empty inside. His life used to have purpose and meaning. He'd fought to protect his country and keep its streets safe. He'd helped people, but now he was the one who needed help. He knew that, and maybe someday he would see about getting some, but not now.

"Not until I finish what I started," he renewed his vow.

The wind whistled a shrill scream, slapping icy rain against the window. Bob took a step back, feeling like someone had slapped him across the face for daring to voice his opinion. No one believed his theories. They thought he was crazy. Obsessed, they'd said, for being unwilling to let the case go. Something about politics and having to play nice with the other law enforcement agencies to keep the peace. What happened to fighting for truth and justice at any cost? Didn't anyone care that a woman had died? An accident they'd said.

Bull-fucking-shit was what *he'd* said.

The next day he'd received his walking papers, pulled from the case, confined to desk duty. He let out a harsh laugh. *Bull-fucking-shit.* He shook his head in defeat. Not long after that, they forced him into early retirement, *for his own good*, mind you. Several flashes of lightning streaked across the sky, and for a moment he wondered if he'd passed out again. Maybe this was just a psychedelic dream. A boom of thunder cracked so loud it rattled the window, assuring him he was fully awake and matching the storm's mood.

Anger. Fury. Resentment.

Retiring at fifty-five hadn't done him a damn bit of good. Being an agent was all he knew. He'd worked too fucking hard to go out this way. What the hell was he supposed to do? He hadn't been able to cope and had turned to whiskey and taking matters into his own hands. Shit, maybe he had been a little obsessed back then, but for good reason. Too bad his wife hadn't thought so. He raised the bottle and drained the last of the liquid, admitting he still was obsessed and a little worried his passion would fade someday. Because, if his obsession faded....

What would he have left?

Picking up a picture of his ex-wife and his little boy, his eyes filled with moisture. He'd known from the second he'd met her when he was on an assignment in Hawaii that she was *The One*. Long dark-chocolate hair, cocoa eyes, and tanned skin: she'd been the most beautiful woman he'd ever seen. Still was, even though she'd moved on and remarried. Didn't matter. He would always love her. And their little boy looked just like her, except his eyes were hazel—a mix of Bob's green eyes and her brown.

He set the picture down and glanced up into the mirror before him, startling himself for a moment. He'd aged horribly in the last ten years, a mere shell of his former self: thin, balding sandy-blond hair, puffy faded green eyes, and wrinkles. So many wrinkles. Abusing alcohol would do that to a person. He knew that, but he couldn't stop drinking any more than he could stop thinking about that case. He hadn't given up, but his hands were "officially" tied for now. *Unofficially* he would do whatever he damn well pleased. All he needed was a little luck. Some new information. A lead. Anything that would help him crack what had become his life's work. Somehow, someway, he would prove them all wrong...

Or fucking die trying.

* * *

"SEE, IT'S NOT SO BAD," Stacy Buchanan said to herself as she pulled into the parking lot of the marina at Coldwater Cove, in the northern part of Maine, and killed the engine to her Prius.

3

Her hometown was a small, seaside fishing village with a humid continental climate consisting of cold snowy winters and warm summers. She remembered well the severe nor'easters that would hit between November and March, striking fear into the bravest of sailors. Tourists knew enough to stay far away, but summer was great. As a consolation to their awful winters, direct strikes from hurricanes or tropical storms during the summer were rare this far north because of the cooler Atlantic waters. That time of year had always been Stacy's favorite. Summer meant her town came alive with people, fishermen filled their boats, and she got to swim in the ocean.

Stacy had thought about her town a lot over the years. Coldwater Cove might be a picturesque little fishing village, but fish weren't the only thing abundant in the summer. Tourists came from all over during the warm weather months on their tour of Maine's breathtaking coast, providing most of the town's revenue. Because, once the brutal winter came, the Cove turned into a dark and desolate ghost town. It was just far enough north that the sun rose and set early, and the harsh weather caused most folks to hibernate.

Late spring could be iffy in Coldwater Cove. Snow turned to rain, the ground grew soggy from the winter's melt, and flooding was sometimes a problem. Remembering the fall, she pictured the various shades of orange and yellow and red leaves, vibrant and gorgeous, dotting the landscape like paint on an artist's canvas. Looking around now, she sighed. Spring was a different story. Everything was bare and colorless, but at least it wasn't depressing like the stale and stagnant days of winter. Spring offered hope of new life to come. Rebirth.

A fresh start.

Clinging to that, Stacy scanned her desolate surroundings as she stepped out of her car, pulled up her hood, zipped up her lined raincoat, and tucked her jeans into her rubber boots. The tourist season hadn't quite picked up yet and most kids were still in school. The day was a dark and gloomy one in the Cove; clouds an ominous gray bulging with rain that had yet to fall, but she didn't care. She could brave it. She was a champion swimmer, after all. While growing up in Coldwater Cove, most of her meets were held indoors. But she had always loved a challenge and swam for miles through the ocean to a few of the many islands offshore, pushing herself to go farther each time.

Her father had called her brave, following along beside her as he drove the media in his charter boat. Her mother had been terrified of the water. She'd never missed an indoor meet but drew the line at watching her daughter put her life at risk in the scary sea. Her mother had always said she wasn't brave like Stacy or her father, that she didn't have their adventurous spirit. Yet it was her mother whose life had ended after she'd braved much more than nasty weather. She'd died in these dark seas ten years ago, yet it seemed like yesterday.

"I can do this." Stacy nodded once, sharply, while setting her jaw.

Inhaling the salty air, she smelled fish and seaweed and pine. Someone had a woodstove going, and a dog barked off in the distance, begging to be let back in. She couldn't blame the poor thing. Even the gulls knew enough to take shelter, leaving the eerie sky bare and calm. Staring out from the quiet cove used to fill her with so much joy. The rugged coastlines consisted of jagged rocks and forested slopes that swept down to the sea as if drowning the coast, while the cliffs were peppered with rocky shores dotted with lighthouses.

Peninsulas had always been her favorite, reaching

out to the sea like old arthritic fingers desperately clinging to life. After her mother's accident, she couldn't help but think of her and how unfair it was that she'd never had the chance to grow old. Stacy often tormented herself by wondering if her mother had reached out with a desperate plea for help in her final moments, only to have her hands come up empty.

Stacy's stomach churned like the water before her as she walked to the edge and along one of the piers. She shivered as she forced herself to look down at the water. This was the very spot they'd found her mother's bloated body floating. The warm salt water had made her nearly unrecognizable after she'd gone missing a few weeks before that. Stacy pictured her mother sinking to her watery grave in the cold dark sea somewhere and then washing up here, which was still so odd because her mother never went near the water.

Stacy loved the water. It had given so much to her, yet it had also taken far too much away. She felt a tear slip down her cheek. She hadn't been able to stay back then and knew she didn't have it in her to stay now. Too many sad memories had nearly drowned her as well, and she'd felt the town's eyes watching her. What were they waiting for? She didn't have a clue. It had been too much to handle back then, as it was now, but she didn't have a choice. Her father needed her, even though it meant giving up everything she'd worked so hard to achieve.

Forcing herself to think of happier thoughts, she looked up at the horizon and pictured the summer. Soon the weather would warm, and wildflowers would cover the hills with a fresh blanket of hope and a sparkling new summer wardrobe to fill the landscape with a wealth of possibilities. Maple and Oak trees lined the cove, while various types of pine trees further inland made up the forests which covered the mountains. Those, in turn, were bisected by fresh-water rivers and lakes like veins running over the body of land. Her hometown really was a beautiful place when it wanted to be, and a cold dark bitch when it didn't.

"There's my little mermaid," came a scratchy voice from behind her, making her jump out of her Docs.

Ever since her mother had died, this town hadn't felt like home. It unsettled Stacy, made her skittish. This town had no hope, no future without summer, and summer had nothing left for her but bad memories and heartache. Steady footsteps vibrated the dock, re-assuring her. A lump formed in her throat as she thought, *Well, almost nothing left for her.* She smiled a little sadly then forced her lips to tip up into a wide grin before she turned around.

"And there's my captain of the seas." She gave her father a big hug, inhaling his comforting familiar smell--Old Spice After Shave mixed with scents of the sea.

He wrapped his strong arms around her in a mas-sive bear hug that brought tears to her eyes. His mind might be going and age was taking its toll, but he was still her larger-than-life hero. Her mother had been a little bitty thing of a teacher and later the mayor, while her father had been a big, strapping fisherman, who towered over everyone in town. She was smart and so-phisticated while he was a bit rough around the edges, but he had a sense of humor that was infectious. No one thought their love would last, but they'd proven everyone wrong.

He'd been forty-five and her mother forty when they'd finally had their miracle baby after years of try-ing. A cross between the two of them, Stacy's five-eleven height worked to her advantage, giving her long strides in the water, yet neither of them would get to see her become a success. Death had robbed her

7

mother of her body, and now early onset Alzheimer's was robbing her father of his mind.

"How come you didn't go straight to the house first?" He leaned back and studied her with the same amber eyes that she had, but her wild curly auburn hair came from her mother. His hair used to be brown, but had turned silver with age, though it was still as thick as ever.

"I needed to come here first." She swallowed hard and tried not to let her lips tremble.

She hadn't been back in ten years, plenty of time to mourn and move on, yet being home for only a few moments had already brought all the emotions to the forefront. She hadn't counted on her feelings hitting her so hard and reliving everything as if it were yesterday. At first, her father had come to visit her at the University of North Carolina to watch her swim meets, understanding she wasn't ready to return to the Cove without her mother.

And then, he kept coming to visit when she'd graduated in journalism, working for various newspapers and magazines, understanding her drive and ambition when it came to her career was what kept her away longer. He'd only asked her once if she ever thought of settling down and starting a family of her own, but she had seen what the death of her mother had done to him. He'd never remarried or moved on, his broken heart still evident to this day. Stacy wanted no part of that. She'd always been Daddy's little girl, and he knew her better than she knew herself.

He'd never asked again.

"I understand," he said in a quiet voice filled with gravel as he brushed a stray curl behind her ear, the words *it doesn't get any easier* left unspoken, but she knew they were both thinking it.

He had no idea coming home meant giving up her

dream job of working for ESPN. The company did most of its broadcasting in Connecticut, but they had an office in North Carolina, and they'd made her an offer just after his doctor had called. When it came to her father, there was no question of what her decision would be. He'd given her everything and had been there for her, always. He still was. He was her rock and now she needed to be his, though he stubbornly refused to admit he needed help.

"What I don't understand is why you're out here alone, Dad." She crossed her arms and stared him down, needing to focus on something other than herself.

"I'm old, not dead." He shoved his big hands in the pockets of his raincoat. "And last time I checked I still had a brain."

"No one's saying you don't," she responded gently. "It's just not safe. What if you get confused again?"

She'd noticed his forgetfulness for a while but had thought it was a simple part of growing old. Until the doctor had called her after the police found him miles away, up the coast with no idea where he was or how he had ended up there. Once they brought him home, he remembered, but he hadn't been the same since; and sadly, more episodes had occurred.

"That's why I have this here fancy gadget." He patted his chest with gnarled, brown-spotted fingers. "I don't have to remember who to call. All I have to do is press this button, and someone will come help. Doc gave it to me."

Relief took the edge off of her emotions. Dr. Hurn had been a friend of both her parents, and Stacy trusted her judgment. If the doctor thought Stacy's father was still okay out alone, then that was good enough for her. "Good. I'm glad to see you're wearing it."

"I might be stubborn, but I ain't stupid," he grumbled while standing a little straighter. "So how long are you here for?"

"The summer," she couldn't quite meet his eyes, "then I'll figure things out after we sell the house and get you settled."

Even with not meeting his eyes, she could see him set his jaw. "I don't want to live somewhere else, Stac, and I wouldn't have to if you moved back home. That house was your mother's and my first home. It's where you were conceived and born. You grew up there. How am I supposed to throw all that away?"

"It also has haunting memories, Dad. It's not the same with Mom gone, and I can't stay. It's too hard."

She pressed her lips into a flat line, trying to pull herself together. She'd tried to get him to leave with her, but he'd refused to let go of the only place he'd ever called home. She knew the real reason. He refused to let go of her mother.

"I have a life I'm building," she went on. "A career I eventually need to get back to, and you can't take care of that house by yourself. Not to mention, you need help to remember your medicine, among other things. The assisted living complex Gary Sanders told me about sounds perfect. It's right in town and close to everything." She squeezed his hand. "It's *not* a nursing home, Dad. You still have all your independence and freedom, and I promise I will come back to visit often this time."

"Let's not talk about you leaving already. You just got here. I've got a pot of chowder on, and the coffee's brewing." He studied the sky with amber eyes so like her own. "It's gonna be a doozy of a storm, and it's going to start right...about...now!"

Just like that the heavens opened up. Fat raindrops splattered down on them, daring them to escape the punishment. He'd always had an uncanny way of reading the weather from his years spent out at sea. Some things might be fading away from his brain, but he was still a sailor through and through.

He held out his arm in a crook, and Stacy started laughing as she snaked her hand through the loop like she used to when she was little. They dashed for the cover of her car, just like old times, albeit at a slightly slower pace. Her smile faded as an odd sense of foreboding drifted over her, whispering eerily on the cold wind that *nothing* was like old times and things would never be the same again. A storm was brewing, all right, but only time would tell how bad the aftermath would be.

* * *

STACY BUCHANAN WAS BACK!

I stood in the shadows of a boat docked in the cove, watching, waiting. My gaze kept scanning the harbor, looking for others, but no one was foolish enough to venture out in this weather. Not even the fisherman, whose boats nestled snugly against the dock, ready for whatever Mother Nature doled out. Cinching the hood of my dark coat tighter, I shoved my hands in my pockets, striving for patience. I was close. Thirty steps away, and she had no clue. It would be so easy to do what I had done before, to let history repeat itself. My head hurt from trying to calculate the odds of discovery.

I wasn't born a killer, didn't have the stomach for it. But desperation could make a person do things they never dreamed were possible. And living with what I had done had gotten easier over the years because I had been justified. That was why I hadn't gotten caught. I had gotten away with it once. Maybe I could again. Maybe I was justified once more. I damn sure knew I was desperate after hearing the rumors around town. I

11

hadn't believed the gossip until she'd driven right by me. Of course I followed her. My eyes darted everywhere at once as my heartbeat sped up and my pulse raced. I balled my hands into fists.

After ten years of staying away, she'd had to fucking come back!

Why? Because of her old man? Maybe I should get rid of him, too, then she would never have a reason to come back. I couldn't have her in town now or ever. Not after everything that had happened, what I'd had to go through to get where I was today. I'd worked too goddamned hard. I'd heard she was a journalist now. Journalists were nosy. The last thing I needed was her poking her nose in where it didn't belong by digging up the past. I had to do something. I couldn't risk the truth being revealed. I pulled on my gloves, knowing this was it, and looked up to take a step forward.

Shit!

When had her father shown up? The sky spit fat raindrops in fair warning for the curtains of water about to fall, and then they were climbing into the shelter of her car. I'd missed my chance. I stepped back into the sopping shadows, trying not to let my paranoia cripple me. Calming myself with deep breaths, determination and resolve settled over me. I would be smart about this. I would do whatever was necessary to protect what was mine, just like before. I might have missed my chance at this moment, but make no mistake, there would be other chances. I didn't have a choice anymore.

Stacy Buchanan must leave town or die...

Because I couldn't stop until this nightmare was finished.

2

TRENT CLARK PULLED his Worldwide Parcel Service truck up in front of the rundown old New Englander on Maple Drive. The white paint was peeling, a few of the spindles on the front porch rotting, and the yard was in desperate need of some tender loving care. The storm last night had knocked down branches and blown debris all over the already disastrous yard. He could only imagine what the inside looked like. The house sat on the outskirts of town near the water yet far enough away not to be considered waterfront. Trent had always had a love of architecture and remodeling old homes. This one held so much potential, it was a shame to see it fade away from its former glory.

Shrugging, he picked up his clipboard. He wasn't here to assess this house, he was here to deliver a package to its owner. Glancing at the name on the package list, he blinked in surprise. Stacy Buchanan. Trent hadn't lived in Coldwater Cove for long, only about six months, but he knew the story of Elizabeth Buchanan's untimely death a decade ago. The townsfolk had been divided on how they felt. She had as many enemies as she did friends, and the toll her death had taken on her husband was downright sad. Trent genuinely liked Mack Buchanan. He had delivered pretty regularly to him recently, but there had never been anything for his daughter. Trent glanced beyond the side of the house and could just make out a car he didn't recognize.

Gathering up the package, he stepped out of his truck into the calm stillness of the storm's aftermath and walked down the cracked driveway. Scents of damp earth mixed with the salty sea drifted to his nose. Bypassing the front door, Trent headed toward the garage. He'd come to discover that, while all the houses in Maine had a front door, very few of the homeowners used them. In fact, a lot of the houses didn't even have a sidewalk that led to the front door because all the visiting townsfolk knew to come in through the back entrance. Parcel carriers were no exception.

Trent knocked and heard the distinct hoarse male voice he'd come to know well holler, "Come in," without having a clue who was on the other side. Trent turned the knob and stepped inside.

As a former Marine, having served for eight years right out of high school and seen too many awful things while doing so, trusting didn't come easy for Trent. Knowing pretty much everyone in town kept their doors unlocked was something he would never get used to. Then again, he didn't plan to reside here permanently, and being a parcel carrier was just one of many jobs he'd held on his road to discovering the truth. Ever since getting out of the military nine years ago, he'd been on a mission of another kind. One he couldn't tell anyone about, not even the people closest to him, which often led to long days and lonely nights.

"Now there's a strapping young lad if ever I've seen one." Mack held out his large hand and shook Trent's.

Trent was a big guy, standing six-two with muscles he'd spent years building, but this man was huge. He had to be at least six-seven, with a thick, broad-shouldered frame that was still impressive, even with muscles withering a bit from age and fingers gnarling with arthritis from years of reeling in fish. It was a damn shame to watch the man's mind go first when his body was still so strong.

"While I appreciate that, sir, have you looked in the mirror?" Trent chuckled. "I don't think I've ever seen a man as impressive as you."

"Should've seen me in my youth." Mack winked, then rubbed his hands together as if they were sore. "Growing old's no fun, boy, but enough of the depressing talk." He studied the package. "Whatcha got for me?"

"Actually, it's not for you." Trent double-checked the name. "It's for a Stacy Buchanan." He looked up at Mack curiously. "I'm assuming she's your daughter?"

"That she is. Got my eyes and height, but she's smart like her mother," Mack said with pride. "Must be from one of those magazines or newspapers she writes for. She's a journalist and a damn good one. Gonna make a big name for herself someday. All she needs is a break. Here, I'll take the package off your hands."

"Sorry, it says she has to sign for it." Trent glanced around the empty house, trying not to seem as eager as he was to lay eyes on the woman he'd read so much about. All the photos of her were ten years old, and he couldn't help wonder how much she had changed since then. "Is she here?"

"She sure is," came a female voice that sounded smooth and warm like honey, reminding him of a talk radio host he'd once heard at a time when he'd needed comfort.

Stacy Buchanan stepped out from behind her father, and Trent couldn't help but stare. She'd grown and matured for the better. Not that her pictures at seventeen

15

were bad, but they sure didn't do the twenty-seven-year-old woman she'd become justice. She stood just under six feet tall, with a swimmer's body of long, lean muscles in all the right places.

She wasn't the most beautiful woman he'd ever seen, but she was unique and interesting with that crazy head of wild auburn curls that somehow worked for her. Yet it was her warm amber eyes that held him captive. They matched that mesmerizing voice of hers, affecting him in ways he hadn't been affected in years. There had been plenty of women, but nothing serious. He'd had no time for relationships. He couldn't risk it. When duty called, he answered. This time was no different.

Masking his physical reaction to her, he forced a neutral expression on his face and held out her package. "Here you go, ma'am. If you could sign for this, I'll be on my way."

"Ma'am was my mother." She took the package from him and smiled. "You can call me Stacy."

He handed her a small electronic device for her to sign with a smile of his own. "Stacy it is." Their fingers brushed, and he felt a spark of electricity he was forced to ignore for both their sakes, but that didn't stop his smile from fading into a slight frown.

She blinked and then cleared her throat as she took the device to sign, and he dropped his hand. "And your name is?" she asked without looking at him, but her fair skin had a pink hue to it that hadn't been there a moment ago.

"This here's Trent Clark," her father boomed and clapped him on the shoulder. "Best parcel carrier in the area. Been making sure I get my meds on time for months now so I don't have to remember to pick them up. He's a real lifesaver, this one."

"Just doing my job, sir."

"Modest, too. He's staying at the old Coswell Cottage just down the road on the water. You should see what he's done to the place. Amazing."

"Just earning my keep."

"Done?" Her eye's sparked with curiosity. "Are you a carpenter, too?"

"It's more of a hobby. I like to buy old houses and renovate them so I can flip them for a profit. Helps pay the bills when my day job isn't enough. The Coswells retired in Florida and rent their cottage out in the summer, but they're thinking of selling it. They let me stay for free if I agreed to fix the place up while I'm here. I couldn't say no to that. Speaking of day jobs, I should run. I have a lot more deliveries to get to before the end of the day." Trent waved to Mack and headed out the door.

"Wait," Stacy said from behind him a few moments later while touching him on the shoulder.

He turned around and a whiff of her perfume engulfed his senses. Damn she smelled good. Like sunshine and flowers and woman. He glanced at his watch, needing to escape before he did or said something stupid. "I only have a minute. Clock's ticking at the office, unfortunately."

"Sorry, this won't take long." She wrung her hands. "I was just wondering if you could help me with something."

"What's that?"

"I'm sure you've probably heard my father is in the early stages of Alzheimer's."

Trent nodded. "Yes, I had. I'm sorry."

"Me too." Her voice filled with a hint of pain, and he had the strongest urge to hug her. He clenched his fists to keep from reaching out for her and focused on what she was saying. "Anyway, he can't live alone much longer," she went on, "and he only has me to help him settle his affairs. Once I secure a safe place for my father to stay, Gary Sanders, the local realtor, is going to help me sell this house. In order to do that, I need to make some repairs, maybe remodel a bit. I've been away for so long, I'm not sure who I can trust to do a good job and be fair. My father seems to trust you, so what do you say? Like you said, it's extra money, and we could work around your schedule."

Trent thought about it. This just might be the perfect solution. He'd been working on getting close to her father, and he needed access to her house, to her mother's things. Maybe getting close to her was the answer he'd been looking for. All the more reason to keep things professional and not cross the line into personal.

He held out his hand. "Done." They shook on it. "When do I start?"

"As soon as possible." She rubbed her arms as if rubbing off the cold, even though the weather was shaping up to be a gorgeous day, making him wonder what exactly had given her chills to begin with. "And thank you."

"You're welcome," he replied and walked away.

She wouldn't be thanking him when she found out the truth. What he was doing was just and right and necessary, he reminded himself, but he couldn't help thinking he'd go to hell for lying. Sometimes he hated the things he was doing, but he knew he would do whatever it took to finish what he'd started.

* * *

THE NEXT DAY, Stacy decided to go through her mother's things. She needed to figure out what to keep and what would go to Goodwill. Gary Sanders was taking her father to look at Whispering Pines. It was an assisted living complex. She'd tried to go with them, but her father had put his foot down, reminding her he was the parent. He still had all his faculties, and he could damn well make his own decisions.

She'd let the matter drop and had stayed home.

He'd relented by agreeing to let her decide on what to keep of her mother's, probably because, in ten years, he hadn't been able to let go of anything of hers. He obviously needed help in more ways than one, and most likely, so did Stacy. This was the hardest thing she'd ever had to do. Not ready to tackle her mother's bedroom yet, she decided to start with her office. She headed in that direction when a knock came at the back door. Grateful for the distraction, she quickly answered.

"Well, hello, Mr. Clark." A genuine smile tipped up her lips.

Trent was a site for sore eyes, so tall and buff and ruggedly handsome. He wore his hair buzzed short, and a five-o'clock shadow blanketed his face. Hazel eyes stared down at her with charming crow's feet creased at the corners, but none of that mattered. She wouldn't stick around long enough to make any of it matter. Good looking or not, she still didn't want to settle down. What she wanted was to get back to her career, and that meant fixing up her father's house and making sure he was okay.

Her brows puckered as a thought came to her. "Wait, shouldn't you be at work?"

"I am." Dressed in beat-up work boots, worn-out blue jeans that fit him oh-so-perfectly, and a faded t-shirt that hugged his muscles and brought out the green in his hazel eyes, he held up his toolbox. "I had the day off, so I thought I would get a start on my second job if you don't mind. You did say ASAP, right?"

"Absolutely." She stepped aside. "By all means, come

right in." He walked through the door, set down his toolbox, and looked around. "How bad is it?"

"Well, it's not as bad as I thought compared to the outside, no offense." He walked all through the house with her at his heels, studying everything, then he came to a stop where he'd started.

"Believe me, none taken." She sighed. "I thought the same thing when I first got home. What are you thinking as far as repairs? My father says he has plenty of money, and his lawyer confirms it. I say he might as well spend it on something useful."

"For starters, you'll need to scrape the peeling paint away on the outside to restore it to its former glory. I know a crew. There's a couple of spindles that need to be replaced on the front steps and a few floorboards. That would be a good place for me to start."

"Okay, what about the inside. Any thoughts? As a person who's spent her life training and swimming and studying, I've never been very girlie. I can't cook, have no idea how to decorate, and don't even get me started on what is or isn't in fashion. To say I need help would be a major understatement."

"I don't know," he looked her over with a twinkle in his eye, "I think you look great, so you must be doing something right. As for cooking and decorating, I've got you covered."

He stepped forward and studied the area, thank God. Stacy fanned her cheeks, hoping they would cool before he saw her blush over his compliment. It didn't help that he smelled great, like sandalwood and soap and man. That only made her face flame hotter. She really needed to get a grip and focus.

"This entryway is really closed in and kind of dark," he went on, forcing her to pay attention. "Since it doesn't lead to anywhere, I would suggest removing the wall right here between the foyer and living room. That will create a bright open space."

"That's a great idea."

"And I would go with white paint for all the interior walls. Pale colors make a space look bigger and look like a blank canvas full of possibilities to potential buyers. You can add fancy molding, corner bookcases and shelves, and new lighting. The hardwood floors will need to be refinished for sure. What's upstairs—other than two bedrooms, I'm guessing?" He glanced at her and raised a brow curiously.

She stopped fanning her cheeks and dropped her hands, trying not to look stupid. "Just an unfinished attic. Any thoughts about that?"

He stopped staring at her flushed cheeks, much to her relief, and looked pensive. "You could add on to the home by turning the attic into a master suite for anyone with a bigger family."

"That sounds perfect." He really had an amazing eye. She wouldn't have imagined doing any of that. "Anything else?"

"I would put a window seat right there." He pointed to an area off her dining room that faced the back yard. "You could add more cabinets for lots of storage with a butcher block countertop right here between the kitchen and dining room. It can serve as an island with more seating for meals."

"I love window seats."

Stacy could just imagine curling up in a nook like that while reading a good mystery romance. A pang of sadness over selling her childhood home surprised her. She hadn't expected to feel any remorse about moving on, but she did. As much as she had run from her past over the last decade, that didn't mean she didn't care or miss it a little bit. "I know this place is old, but is there anything worth saving?" Maybe if they could keep a piece of her past, this whole process would be easier.

"I would hold onto the vintage features like this big beam in the kitchen and some antique pieces I'm assuming your mother chose. She had a good eye," he said softly as though guessing at Stacy's nostalgic mood. He hooked a thumb over his shoulder toward the back of the house. "But that steep staircase in the back room has to go. You can add a mudroom since everyone in this town comes in through the back of the house anyway." He scrubbed a hand over his jaw. "I still can't believe you people don't lock your doors."

"Oh, trust me, I'm not *you people* anymore. I've lived away long enough to learn the value of locking one's door, but my father is old-school. He wants his house welcome to all, no matter how many times I try to reason with him."

"I've come to see that for myself over the past six months. He and his fellow former captains meet for coffee down at the pier. I've overheard a few of their conversations. They are a tough bunch and stubborn as the day is long."

"Exactly." She huffed out a breath. "Okay, Mr. Clark. It sounds like we have a ton to do. Where do you want me first?"

"Mr. Clark was my father." He grinned, throwing her words back at her. "You can call me Trent. I've got my end covered down here. I'll need to make some calls, take some measurements, and draft up a plan." He glanced toward the ceiling. "If you want to help, you could start by cleaning out the attic."

Stacy wilted in relief. That meant she got to put off going through her mother's office for one more day. Everything important had already been gone through by the police and hauled away, but there were her mother's personal things still to be dealt with. "I'm on it," she said. "Holler if you need me. Oh, and feel free to use my mother's office. There's a phone in there, and she has a great desk." Stacy could have sworn she saw a flash of something enter his eyes, but it was gone so quickly she'd probably imagined it.

"Thanks," he said and disappeared from view.

She shrugged off her suspicion, knowing this town had a way of clouding her judgment. Trent Clark had been great to her father and a lifesaver to her so far, she reminded herself as she headed up the stairs.

Then why did she have the strangest feeling he was hiding something?

23

3

"I WON'T LIKE IT," Mack said to Gary Sanders while staring out the passenger window of Gary's new luxury sedan. Fully loaded, with leather seats and that new car smell of money.

Gary had been a part of Coldwater Cove almost as long as Mack had, and they'd both suffered the loss of a loved one, with Mack's wife and Gary's son having passed away only a year apart. They'd never been close friends, but over the years they'd formed a bond of mutual respect and empathy. While Gary had picked himself up and turned his life around, becoming a well-respected member of the community and a successful realtor, Mack had never really found the strength or will to move on.

Gary sighed. "Give it a shot, Mack. Whispering Pines is just beyond the cove in the heart of town, situated on beautiful grounds with access to just about anything you might ever want or need. You will be able to come down and watch the boats any time you want. Not to mention there are some great people living there. You might make a few new friends. This town helped me when I needed them the most. Let me do the same for you. It's time you start letting folks in again."

"I'm too old and set in my ways, Gary, but I appreciate your concern. I'll keep an open mind for Stacy, but I'm not making any promises."

"Fair enough." Gary glanced at him, looking him up and down with a raised brow. "And for the record, you're not that much older than me."

Mack studied Gary. He was average height and still in decent shape, with all his teeth and salt and pepper hair that accented his fancy suits perfectly. All in all, a good-looking healthy man who'd been through a lot and had risen above tragedy. He was one of the lucky ones.

"I got you by more than a decade," Mack said ruefully, "and you're not the one losing his mind."

Gary chuckled. "That's debatable these days, my friend. Summer tourist season will be picking up, and you know how that goes."

"A few more gray hairs and wrinkles every year mixed with a whole lot of crazy." Mack smiled fondly as he thought of the past. "I used to thrive on that hazy, hot chaos. Summer meant open water and big fish and chartering tourists. It meant money in my bank account and money for this town." His smiled faded a bit. "It meant watching my baby girl swim the channel like a little mermaid. Man, I miss those days."

"I hear that. My boy Chase was sure something, wasn't he? I used to love to watch him run like the wind. Indoor sprints, outdoor cross country, there wasn't anything he couldn't do when it came to running."

"That he was. Put Coldwater Cove on the map with all the records he set. Elizabeth sure took a shine to that boy. Then again she loved helping all the young athletes in the Cove get their big break. She would have been so proud of both him and Stacy getting full scholarships to college. It's a shame his life was cut so short."

Gary's face grew somber. "Same with your wife. Accidents are tragic, don't you think? They have a way of sneaking up and blindsiding you when you least expect it. Turns a person's whole world upside down."

Mack nodded. "That's what makes them hard to get over."

"Well, we're here." Gary's tone made it clear he was glad to change the depressing subject as he put the car in park and opened his door. "You ready?"

"No." Mack climbed out. "But I'll give it a whirl anyway."

"You're making the right decision."

"Seems like I don't have a choice."

"Sometimes we all have to do things we don't want to. Chalk it up to the necessary evils of life, but you'll be better for it in the end."

"Time will tell." Mack followed Gary into the complex, but he couldn't shake the feeling that his residence wasn't the only thing about to change in this town, and he wasn't at all sure that anyone would be better because of it.

* * *

LATE THAT NIGHT, Stacy couldn't put it off any further. It was time. Her father was dozing in his easy chair in the living room with the TV on, and she couldn't sleep. She made her way to her mother's office and stepped inside. Even after ten years, she could still smell her mother, feel her presence in this room that had been such a big part of her mother's life. Memories of when Stacy was little brought a lump to her throat.

She used to sit under her mother's desk to be near her, be a part of her mysterious world, and color pictures of the ocean. Her mother never minded. She knew Stacy was closer to her father and was a huge

26

part of his world, so she treasured whenever Stacy showed an interest in spending time with her. As much as her mother didn't like the water, she would praise Stacy's drawings and hang her pictures with pride. The last one Stacy had drawn was still displayed on the wall behind her mother's desk.

Going through her senior year had been hard for Stacy with her mother gone. She'd missed so much: having her mother help her shop for a prom dress; having her mother attend her signing to a Division 1 school for swimming; having her mother watch her graduate high school with honors. Her father had been heartbroken and sad. He'd done the best he could with Stacy, but it just wasn't the same without her mother. By college he'd become her rock, but he was still heartbroken and sad to this day.

Stacy didn't know where to start.

The FBI had combed over her mother's office, looking for something. They never did say what, but they had started investigating her about something to do with her job as the mayor of Coldwater Cove before her death. Stacy had only been seventeen. Too young to really know much about politics, but not too young to know the town had been divided when her mother was elected as mayor. She wanted to clean up the streets and make her town safe for her only daughter, and that didn't sit well with the large gun-toting, hunting, and gambling crew. But her mother also did a lot for the youth of Coldwater Cove that didn't go unnoticed.

In Stacy's eyes, her mother was a hero.

Elizabeth Buchanan was a strong, independent woman to be admired and looked up to. The cops had tried to say otherwise, and that wasn't okay with Stacy's father. They'd started looking into both her and his comings and goings in the harbor suspiciously. He hated cops because of it; therefore, so did she. But that didn't stop the niggling doubts that plagued her now that she was an adult herself.

Had her mother or father been involved in something illegal that she had been too young to know about? The FBI wouldn't have been there otherwise. Or had her mother been an innocent party, trying to help them get to the bottom of something that was bigger than any of them realized? And what about her father? There wasn't much that went on in the harbor that he didn't know about.

After her mother's death was ruled an accident and the case closed, the FBI went away. Anything worth finding had already been found, so Stacy had assumed that meant there was nothing to *be* found. Case closed. End of story. So why had her niggling doubts started up again the second she came home? Shaking off her unease, she decided to forget about things she couldn't do anything about and focus on something she could— like sorting through her mother's personal belongings.

Stacy spent the next hour packing up boxes of pictures, drawings, little knickknacks she'd made for her mother during school, and anything else that was purely personal and not simple office fare. The office items that she could donate or sell, she set aside. Finally feeling as though she might be able to get some sleep, she stood up from her mother's desk and was about to head for the door but then stopped in her tracks.

On a sidebar her mother had placed by the door, she'd displayed a clock Stacy had made for her in Wood shop. Stacy smiled fondly, remembering how much her mother had loved that clock. That was one item Stacy decided to keep for sure. She walked slowly over and picked up the clock, examining it from every angle. It had withstood the test of time fairly well. Biting her bottom lip, she stared at the secret compartment she'd added in the bottom. She and her mother used to pass special little notes of love and affection to each other through that compartment. It was their treasured secret that no one knew about, not even her father.

Fighting back tears, Stacy opened the compartment and blinked, her jaw falling slack. Her pulse raced. There was a note inside. Had her mother written her one final message before she died? With pounding heart and trembling fingers, Stacy unfolded the piece of paper and then frowned. What on earth? It wasn't a love note from mother to daughter, it was a note from some anonymous person to Stacy's mother. Written in cut-out letters glued onto a piece of paper, serial-killer style, the note said:

IF YOU TELL *what you know, so will I. We need to talk. If you don't want your career ruined,*

meet me at Mariner's Marina on the old, abandoned pier up the coast at sundown

tonight. Tell no one where you're going, or there will be consequences.

STACY'S MOUTH fell open on a gasp and she stared in shock, rereading the note several times. Someone must have been blackmailing her mother. It had to have been pretty serious if they were able to lure her near the water. By putting the note in their secret hiding place, her mother must have figured if she didn't make it home, the note would be found.

Stacy had been so distraught; she couldn't bring herself to touch anything personal of her mother's after she went missing. It had been too painful. Yet she'd never gotten over the feeling that something was off when they'd said her mother's death was an accident. She hadn't felt safe in her hometown ever since. And now she had to live with the guilt that maybe she could have done something if only she had looked harder. She was the only one who could have found the note and saved her mother in time, but she'd let her down and her mother had died because of it.

Stacy would never stop blaming herself.

She wiped away a tear and studied the note again. It was dated the same day her mother had disappeared. Her mother had said she'd had a few errands to run, but she hadn't said where she was going and she had never returned. At first there was speculation that she had run off and left them, but anyone who knew her mother well would know she would never do something like that. She had loved her husband and adored her daughter.

Finally, her mother's body was discovered a few weeks later in the Cove, wearing the same clothes she'd had on the night she'd disappeared, minus one shoe. Everyone had assumed she fell in the cove and drowned, getting tangled up in seaweed or something until finally rising to the surface. Maybe she hadn't fallen in. Maybe someone had pushed her. Maybe the old abandoned marina was the key.

Maybe, just maybe, it was time someone discovered the truth.

* * *

THE SEAS WERE calm the next morning, the days growing longer and warmer. The kids would be out of school in a week and the official summer tourist season would start. This was the perfect time to see what she could find. Just like her mother, Stacy told her father she had to run some errands. She knew if she told him she was going to Mariner's Marina, he would get suspicious and wonder why and probably insist on going with her. She wasn't ready to tell him anything until she had proof. He was too fragile emotionally, and she wasn't at all sure he could handle her mother's case being reopened and all that would accompany that. But she also knew she could never rest easy until she had some answers.

She owed her mother that.

Stacy pulled her Prius into the gravel parking lot of the deserted marina, tires crunching in the eerie silence. It was small and abandoned with only four docks to tie boats up to and a rundown shack that used to be a bait shop. After the marina closed a long time ago, people used to park and use it as a boat and watercraft launch while the local teenagers used it as a place to party and make out. Stacy never did. She'd been too focused on training for her sport, but she did remember her father taking her there once, when she was really little, to fish. Now it just seemed creepy, especially thinking this could have been her mother's last view.

Stacy climbed out of her car, carrying her snorkel gear, and walked to the edge of the water. A hawk circled overhead, and something scurried in the nearby grass, probably a rodent seeking a safe haven. She could relate, feeling completely alone and vulnerable. The docks were in dire need of repair because of rotting, weathered wood, and she doubted anyone even knew this spot existed anymore. It wasn't safe, but she would take her chances anyway. Stripping off her clothing, she zipped the wetsuit she'd hidden beneath all the way up. Even though summer was officially here, the water was still cold this far north.

With ginger steps, she carefully made her way down the length of each dock and searched the water. She had no clue what she was looking for after ten years. For all she knew her mother had her meeting here and then left. Maybe she did stop by the cove and fall in somehow. Stacy certainly wasn't finding any evidence of wrongdoing at this marina. A flock of gulls soared overhead, and one swooped down to snag a fish right out of the ocean. The ripples rolled across the placid water. A foghorn sounded way off in the distance, the sound waves emulating those ripples until everything eventually grew peaceful once more.

As peaceful as possible when investigating a cold case murder.

What was she doing here, Stacy wondered? This was probably just a waste of time. She was about to turn back from the last dock and head home when a flash of light caught her eye. She squinted and searched the dark water once more, but didn't see anything. The water wasn't that deep off the edge of the dock, but, just beyond that, the ocean floor dropped off quickly. Another flash of light reflected as a cloud passed over the sun. Stacy could just make out something silver. Probably an old fishing lure, but she'd come this far. She might as well check it out.

Slipping on her snorkel gear, she sat on the end of the dock and lowered herself into the water, careful not to cause too many ripples. She didn't want to lose sight of her treasure. Swimming slowly out over the top of the sea, she headed in the direction of the light and looked down through her mask. Dark green seaweed, orange coral, and fish of all colors swam before her in a graceful ballet.

The water wasn't as clear or blue as the tropics and the fish not as vivid, but the same feeling of peace and being at home swept over Stacy. The mysteries of the ocean made her feel as though she were one with nature, a part of some secret place she was privileged enough to visit. She knew if she respected the power of the sea, it would respect her back, and everything would be okay.

Venturing out to the edge of the drop-off, she spotted the flash again. It looked like a buckle. She took a deep breath and dove down to pull the object free from its nesting place. She gasped in shock when she saw what the object was and swallowed a mouthful of water, bubbles obscuring her view in a curtain of little white foamy balls. Placing her feet on the bottom, she pushed hard while trying not to panic.

Swimming up with rubbery legs, she broke the surface in a coughing fit. Her lungs burned, but she sucked in precious air and took a moment to just breathe. She was alive. Treading water, she examined the object in her hand. A shoe. Swallowing the raw lump in her throat, she realized it was her mother's long lost navy blue shoe with silver buckles.

Swimming back to the dock, Stacy set the shoe on the wood and knew what she had to do. She couldn't let her fear gain the upper hand. Turning around, she swam back out to the drop off, took a big breath like she'd been trained to do, and dove deep. She could hold her breath for a long time, but admittedly, she was a bit out of practice.

Rays of sunlight streamed through the water, lighting her way for a while, but as she swam deeper to search the area, the darkness closed in on her. Ominous shapes swam by in the shadows, reminding her to remain calm and not appear threatening. Her temples began to throb, and she knew she didn't have much time left. Finally, she spotted what she was looking for.

An old boat anchor.

With a pounding heart she tried to lift the anchor, but it was too heavy. It had a slimy rope tied around it, covered in algae. She followed the rope to where it was half buried and pulled on it. After several tugs, it broke free from the dirt. There was a knotted loop the size of a bracelet on the end, with the remains of a stocking with holes in it still caught in the knot. Upon closer inspection, she knew in her gut it was her mother's light gray fishnet stocking. Her shoulders shook with sobs that begged to escape over the thought of her mother tied up and helpless, but deep in the sea was no place to break down.

Pulling herself together, Stacy started kicking for the surface. She'd spent too long down below. Her air started to run out and slowly the world around her began to fade to black. She was close to fainting. She remembered from her training the average person who drowned had six or seven minutes of starving the brain of oxygen before brain damage set in. But skilled swimmers who pushed the limit depleted their oxygen supplies from their blood stream. Fainting for them would be deadly and cause brain damage after only two or three minutes.

Stacy was running out of time.

She couldn't die like her mother. She wouldn't let her beloved sea become her undoing, not to mention her father would never survive another tragedy. She couldn't let go of the anchor. It was fate that she found it after all these years. She couldn't risk the water finally washing it away for good and not getting another shot.

Tunnel vision took over, and her will to live kicked in. She kept kicking harder and harder, but her energy was fading, her body shutting down. She was close. So close to the surface. Reality set in. She knew in her gut she wasn't going to make it. Not many people realized when someone drowned it wasn't like the movies portrayed it. They didn't splash around in a fit of panic. Splashing meant they were still okay. It's when they fell silent with just their eyes staring helplessly either just below or just above water that they were in real trouble.

A splash close by impacted and water surged around her, but she could no longer move. All her efforts were for naught, she thought, as the anchor slipped from her hand. Something grabbed her wrist. She tried to use what little energy she had left to fight it off to no avail. It was all too much. She gave up the fight and went limp, her body weightless, wondering if her mother had felt this way. Suddenly Stacy broke through the surface and gasped for breath, coughing up salty water once more. She took a moment to breathe and recover until she realized she wasn't floating on her back. She was being carried through the water. Blinking her eyes open, she looked up in a panic which faded to intense relief as she stared at the face of her angel rescuer.

Trent Clark.

"What? You? How?" Her voice came out a hoarse rasp.

"You're lucky I was in the area." His voice sent vibrations through her body being held so tightly against his impressive chest. "I was making a delivery when I saw your car drive down that old road," he continued. "No one else drives a Prius around here. After I finished my delivery, I drove along the road out of curiosity. I've never delivered anything this way, so I wondered what was down here."

"Not much," she responded, still half in a daze over all that had just happened.

"Exactly." His hazel gaze bore into hers. "Imagine my surprise when I saw your car still there, but you were nowhere around. Then I noticed this random shoe that looked as though it had seen much better days sitting on the end of the dock. Next thing I knew I spotted someone struggling and then floating just beneath the surface. Needless to say I panicked and dove in, clothes and all. Don't know what I'll tell my employer." A muscle in his jaw flexed. "What the hell were you thinking coming out to a place like this alone?"

"I'm a swimmer," she said, her voice sounding weak.

"Not at the moment," he responded dryly.

"Okay, so I'm a bit rusty and overdid it." She felt like a fool.

"That's putting it mildly." He carried her out of the water and didn't set her down until he reached safe dry ground.

"It was stupid. I know better than this," she admitted, holding her beach towel up to him but he wrapped it tightly around her instead.

"Then what on earth could possibly make you do it?" He stood with his hands on his hips and water running in rivulets down his face. His brown shorts and button up short sleeve shirt clung to his muscled frame, making him look somehow even more powerful.

She swallowed, feeling the full impact of his intimidating stare. "That shoe." She pointed to the dock, her finger shaking.

He ground his jaw. "An old shoe made you risk your life?"

"Not just any old shoe." She inhaled a deep breath and tried to dislodge the lump in her throat. "The shoe my mother was wearing the night she went missing."

"Oh." The wind whooshed out of his chest, and the frustration left his face. "What does it mean, then?"

"That my mother didn't die by accident." Stacy fought back the urge to cry and thrust her chin into the air as she squared her shoulders. "She was murdered. The shoe isn't the only thing I found. It was near an anchor, and if I'm not mistaken, it had her stocking wrapped up in the knot. That was why it took so long for her to surface and float down the coast to the bay. Someone tied an anchor to her ankle but then her shoe fell off on the way down, and eventually her foot slipped out and her stocking ripped, setting her free. The autopsy report had clearly stated that she'd drowned, which can mean only one thing."

His tanned face paled and his eyes filled with sympathy as he voiced her worst fears. "Your mother was buried alive in a watery grave."

4

TRENT PULLED his WPS truck into the parking lot at
Coldwater Cove Marina the next morning. An eerie
fog hovered over the water, blanketing the cove in a
shroud of mystery. Stacy made him promise not to tell
her father or anyone else what she had found and not
to go after the anchor by himself. She wanted to do
some research first and come up with a plan to safely
retrieve it, before opening a can of worms and getting
the entire town all riled up right before the summer
tourist season. She'd taken the shoe with her. Mayor
Zuckerman would not be happy, not to mention she
didn't much care for cops. That didn't mean he could
stop thinking about the fact that she had proof her
mother had been murdered. The mayor's death hadn't
been an accident like everyone thought.

His heart twisted and the tension between his
shoulders increased from stress. He needed to finish
what he started before all sorts of law enforcement
got involved, but first things first. He still had a job to
do. Picking up a package for the harbormaster, Trent
climbed out of his truck and headed over to the small
cramped office on the waterfront. The air was still
and thick, dampening his skin as he climbed the steps.

He rapped on the open door and poked his head inside.

Charlie Wentworth looked up. "Hey, Trent. How are you, son?"

Charlie was in his mid-sixties with snow white hair and a pot belly that was straining the seams of his khaki uniform. He was nearing retirement and about as laid back as they came, his duck boots propped on his desk and crossed at the ankles.

"I'm great, how 'bout yourself?"

Trent scanned the messy office and wondered how Charlie found anything with his total lack of organization. There was a pair of binoculars covered in dust that looked as though it had been years since they'd been touched, let alone used to peer out the window and keep watch over the harbor. Then again he probably kept his office that way on purpose so he would have to do as little as possible. He wasn't very motivated and far too old-school in thinking our country was safe.

Coldwater Cove bordered Canada, and Nova Scotia was right across the bay. With so much of Maine being remote, there weren't enough border patrol agents to plug all the holes. Inspection stations and checkpoints were so spread out that many went unmanned for hours. Even with cameras and motion sensors in place, if an illegal immigrant or terrorist slipped through and was seen, he or she would be long gone by the time the agents got there.

"Oh, the old arthritis has been acting up a bit," Charlie rubbed his knees, "but with warmer weather coming, I should be right as rain soon."

"With warmer weather comes increased security I would imagine. You never know who might wander into town during the tourist season. These days large gatherings of people make easy targets to inflict terror."

Trent silently cursed. He hadn't meant to take a dark turn so quickly in their conversation. They didn't know each other that well, and he didn't want Charlie growing suspicious of him.

"Bah, our town's too small. Places like Boston might have to worry more about that, but not us. We'll be fine." The way Charlie said that sounded somehow off, but Trent couldn't quite put his finger on what was wrong.

"If you say so," Trent responded casually. "I would imagine that you would know more than me, having lived here all your life."

Trent said what he knew the harbormaster wanted to hear, but Trent knew all about how growing complacent and too comfortable led to danger. He'd witnessed far too much of that during his last tour in Afghanistan. Here in the states the northern border was a threat that too many people didn't take seriously enough. The Royal Canadian Police and the Canadian Security Intelligence Service had all they could do to keep up with security given their country's refugee laws. People of all sorts claimed asylum and got lost in the system.

"So, what do you have for me today?" Charlie uncrossed his ankles and dropped his boots to the floor, jarring Trent from his thoughts. It took a moment for the old man to unfold his hefty body and stand upright.

"Just one box today." Trent set the box on Charlie's desk so the poor guy wouldn't have to bend over. "If you could just sign here." Trent handed his digital signature box to the elderly man, realizing he wouldn't be much of a deterrent in his current condition even if a criminal did happen to slip through.

Charlie signed and handed the device back. "Thank you kindly. You have a good day now, and stay out of trouble."

"Will do." Trent grinned and tipped his head before walking out the door.

He had almost made it back to his truck when he spotted the forty-seven-foot search and rescue Coast Guard boat pull into the harbor and dock. He climbed into his WPS truck so he wouldn't raise suspicion by just standing there and staring. Once he was inside, he reached for his own set of binoculars.

A crew of four men dressed in orange jackets secured the boat, while the person in charge went in to talk to the harbormaster. Moments later, the man reappeared carrying the same box Trent had just dropped off. The man from the Coast Guard looked around the harbor carefully, then climbed back onto the boat. Shortly thereafter, the crew untethered the vessel and made their way out to sea once more.

Trent watched them until they disappeared from view. He narrowed his eyes in thought. So much of Maine's rocky coast was unpopulated, and the water was deep close to the shore. With Nova Scotia right across the bay, any savvy illegal immigrant, smuggler, or terrorist who knew these waters could get in with little or no detection. There were so many places for small fishing vessels to hide, making it nearly impossible for the Coast Guard to watch over all the open water. Their station was at the end of one of the islands and usually they patrolled larger harbors, so what were they doing in Coldwater Cove?

More importantly, what was in that box?

* * *

BOB SAT in his favorite coffee shop in Boston, nursing a hangover, staring out at the gentle waves rolling across the ocean as if even they knew he couldn't take any more battering. The heavy fog finally began to clear.

Last night was a rough one. He'd gotten into another argument with his son. Lately they went for weeks without speaking and when they did, it usually ended in a fight. His son would plead with him to stop drinking, pull his act together, and find something to live for again so he could enjoy his retirement. Bob would usually get pissed off, telling him he had something the live for—the case—and that the Bureau could fuck his retirement until he proved them all wrong.

He sighed and scrubbed a hand over his thin hair, frowning when he came away with a few strands. He'd lost even more recently. When had that happened? His shoulders wilted and he pinched the bridge of his nose, closing his gritty eyes. He didn't mean to take it out on his boy. He knew his son only meant well. He was worried about his old man; that was all. That was enough. Enough to make the guilt eat away at Bob. Sometimes he wondered if maybe he should give up what had become his life's obsession. Maybe he should stop chasing a lost cause. He'd waited ten years for something—anything—to happen, but had only been left with a cold harsh emptiness.

Nothing to prove that Elizabeth Buchanan had been murdered.

"Excuse me," came a rich, silky voice that sounded somehow oddly familiar. "Are you Special Agent Robert West?"

Bob's eyes flew open, and his chest tightened. He was almost afraid to look. Searching his mind, he tried to remember the evening before. Had he done something he shouldn't have? Lord only knew.

"Mr. West?"

He dropped his hand from his face and looked up at her from his small table by the window. He sucked in a sharp breath. It couldn't be. He looked closer. It was her! She had grown close to his six-foot height and was older now, but there was no mistaking that wild red hair of hers and haunting amber eyes. They had occupied many of his dreams, knowing he'd failed her when it came to her mother.

"Miss Buchanan?"

"So you *do* remember me." She hesitated but then sat across from him, her voice filled with relief yet uncertainty.

"Course I do. You were just a girl back then and I'm not a cop anymore, but I never forget a face and that voice of yours is pretty hard to miss. Coffee?"

"No, thank you. Are you okay?" She studied his green eyes that he knew were faded and undoubtedly filled with red, then let her gaze wander over his frame that was much more fragile and weak these days.

"I've been better. How 'bout you?"

"The same." She took a deep breath. "That's why I'm here."

"What can I do for you? I didn't think, after what happened, that you would ever want to set eyes on me again." He had to admit she'd piqued his curiosity.

"It's true, I'm not very fond of any form of law enforcement, but I'm also not blind. Even back then I knew you didn't believe my mother's death was an accident any more than I did. Your department was terrible to my father, grilling both him and me, trying to say my mother wasn't the woman we thought she was. That she was involved in something shady that had to do with her office as mayor. And my poor father. You questioned his integrity when you brought his boat into it."

Bob looked down at his wrinkled, weathered hands cradling his coffee mug. It had grown cold and he hadn't even noticed, like he had just been going through the motions. He realized that was what his life had come to. Going through the motions of existing but not really living. He suddenly realized he didn't deserve to.

"I'm not innocent," he admitted, acid hitting the back of his throat. "You should know I was a part of all that in the beginning."

"I know."

Her words were spoken without malice, almost as just a simple observation. Maybe she didn't despise him like he'd always assumed she must. He swallowed the lump in his throat and for the first time, he felt hope that one day she would forgive him and he could make it up to her somehow. He looked up at her as she continued.

"After she died, the FBI suddenly went away. The sheriff said my mother's death was an accident, and the case was closed. I remember thinking that something was off. Why wasn't anyone looking into this? The police were so quick to accuse my mother of wrongdoing and try to taint her reputation, yet they vanished when it came time to try to help her by seeking justice and clearing her name. You were the only one who said you thought her death wasn't an accident."

"I tried. I really did, but no one would listen." His voice cracked. He hated feeling weak. Hated what he had become.

"I admit I was angry at you for a long time for not fighting harder. You just went away like the rest of them, and everyone forgot about my mother and went on with their lives, leaving my father broken and me confused and hurting. It wasn't until I looked into you recently that I realized they forced you to go away and stay away, or else. I'm right, aren't I?"

He grunted harshly. "Early retirement or jail. They didn't leave me with much of a choice. I know it doesn't help much, but I get what you're going through.

My wife left me and I disappointed my son, so I pretty much lost everything as well."

"I'm sorry for that." She paused awkwardly, the clatter of silverware and hum of conversation filling the air, then she seemed to make up her mind about something as she went on with conviction. "That's why I'm here. I need your help."

"With what?" He scratched his head. "As you can probably see, I don't have much to offer nowadays."

"Lucky for you I don't need much." Her gaze bore into his. "I just need someone to trust. Someone who believes in my story and will help me discover what really happened."

"What are you talking about?" His heart sped up. "What happened with what?"

"My mother. She didn't die by accident," Stacy's voice hitched as she finished with, "she was murdered."

Bob's eyes widened and his pulse raced. He felt like he might hyperventilate. "How do you know?"

"I have proof." She reached down to pull a large canvas bag off the floor and set it on her lap.

"But...h-how?" He couldn't take his eyes off the bag, wanting to reach across the table and rip it open.

"Well, I was cleaning out my mother's office—"

He shook his head, his hope deflating faster than a life raft with a hole in it. "I personally went over her office many times. We took everything of importance."

"Not everything. There was a clock I made my mother when I was little. We used to pass secret notes to each other through a trap door that no one knew about, not even my father." She opened her bag and pulled something out. "I found this inside." She reached out and handed him a folded up piece of paper.

With shaking hands, he took the note from her and read it. He swallowed hard, his throat bone dry. It couldn't be. He read it three more times to be sure.

Raising his eyes, he stared at her. "Elizabeth was being blackmailed? Then I was right. She must have been involved in something bigger than any of us thought. Someone needs to check the marina."

"This could be personal," Stacy said, her tone indicating she still wasn't ready to believe her mother was anything less than perfect. "The note doesn't have to be related to her career. My mother was involved with a lot of things in town, not just politics. And I already checked the marina. I found this." Stacy pulled out a battered item, and he instantly knew what it was, his heart constricting for them both.

"Your mother's missing shoe," he said in relief. He wasn't crazy. Emotion welled up, threatening to choke him, but he fought it off as he continued. "I searched everywhere for that." He shook his head sadly as he added, "But a note and a shoe don't prove she didn't fall in the sea by accident. That's not enough to prove she was murdered. I'm sorry."

"Just hear me out. The shoe was under water at the edge of the drop-off at Mariner's Marina. Over the edge of the drop-off, I found an old anchor with a rope attached to it." A strange look crossed her face before she continued. "I tried to retrieve it, but it was too heavy to carry to the surface. If you look, I promise you it will be there. The rope has a loop around the end of it with my mother's stocking still caught inside the knot."

He rubbed his temples, trying to process it all. "But the coroner said your mother died from drowning."

"Exactly." Stacy's lips wobbled. She pressed them together for a moment before continuing. "That means my mother was alive when someone tied that rope around her ankle and threw her into the ocean. They left her there to drown and die alone. I pray she was unconscious at the time because anything else is unthinkable." Inhaling a shaky breath, she blurted, "So are you going to help me or not?"

He just kept rubbing his temples. "Why haven't you gone to the sheriff yet?"

"Because I don't trust them," she said, her frustration evident. "The sheriff's office was the one to declare my mother's death an accident and insist the case be closed."

"Yes, but now you have evidence. They will be forced to reopen the case and investigate it as a homicide."

"So you won't help me then?" When he hesitated, she started gathering her evidence and shoving it back into her canvas bag.

"Look, my hands are tied, Miss Buchanan. I don't work for the FBI anymore. They made it clear if I so much as blink in the direction of Coldwater Cove or have anything to do with investigating Elizabeth Buchanan's disappearance, I will be arrested and prosecuted immediately. Besides, the sheriff's office has a new sheriff since those days. Maybe you'll have better luck this time. I'm sorry."

"Yes you are, Mr. West. They might have forced you out before, but this time there's no denying you're running away. No matter what you say, you still are and always have been a special agent. This case is about more than seeking justice for my mother. It's about proving you were right and seeking vindication for yourself." Stacy stood. "Look at what they've done to you. How can you live with yourself by doing nothing in return?"

He couldn't say anything because he knew she was right. He'd lived for this moment for the past ten years, risked everything for this opportunity, but now that it was here he was terrified he would fail. Alcohol made him vow a lot of things, but harsh reality returned when he was sober. She shook her head sadly as she stared at him with the same expression his son had given him the last time he'd seen him.

Disappointment.

Bob watched her walk out the door. Christ, he needed a drink. He paid his bill and left the coffee shop with the intention of heading straight to the liquor store or the nearest bar. Funny thing how life works. Before he knew it, he was headed in the opposite direction toward the bus station instead. Maybe Stacy Buchanan was right. Maybe it was time he grew some balls and stood up for himself. He owed her that much. He owed his son that much.

He fucking owed himself that much.

5

SHERIFF RORY EVANS sat behind the desk in his office. Newly elected, he was eager to prove himself. Some thought he was too young to be sheriff at thirty-seven, but he would show them he had what it took to get the job done. He had worked hard his entire life to earn this position, and nothing or no one was going to take it away from him.

The sheriff's office consisted of his main office, several cubicles for his officers, an interrogation room, and a few holding cells for prisoners while they were detained until their trial and sentencing. Voices chattered outside his door along with ringing telephones, the snap of staplers, the tap tap tap of papers being straightened, and the clicking of fingers typing up reports.

And he was in charge of it all.

Pride filled him. He was a good man, he told himself daily, hoping that one day he would truly believe it. All he'd ever wanted to be was a cop. He believed in the system, but the system wasn't always easy. He'd had to turn a blind eye a time or two along the way, play the game in order to get ahead. But now that he was finally here, he would make up for it. He would be a good sheriff, move on from all the wrong and start fresh. And he would begin today. Picking up a file on his desk, he started thumbing through their current cases when a knock on his door came.

"Come in," he called out, closing the file and sitting back in his chair, when a woman he never thought he would see again walked through the door.

Stacy Buchanan.

He sat up straighter, his heart hammering inside his chest. She was older now. Undoubtedly wiser. Did she recognize him? He'd been twenty-seven back then, a young ignorant deputy looking for his big break. Sheriff Pratt had been a difficult man to work for. Hard to read and about as oily as they came. You did what he wanted, no questions asked. Against his conscience and better judgment, Rory had complied out of desperation and a burning drive to succeed.

Now, after all these years, his actions might be coming back to bite him in the ass while Pratt enjoyed a hefty retirement in Boca Raton. Figured. The old bastard had never taken the fall for anything in his life, leaving everyone else to clean up his mess. That wasn't likely to change any time soon.

Smoothing a hand over his thick, wavy, light brown hair, Rory smiled at her with all the charm he could muster as he stood. She was only ten years younger than him. Not a big deal at their age. He remembered the way she'd looked at him back then, with stars in her eyes. Although she wasn't really his type—too tall, too athletic, a curly haired redhead—but he didn't have a choice. His baby blues had never let him down before. He was hoping they wouldn't this time since he had a sinking feeling he would need to charm her more than ever.

"Please, have a seat, Miss Buchanan." He gestured to

the overstuffed chair on the other side of his desk. "Can I get you anything? Coffee? Water?"

"No thank you. I wondered if you would remember me," she said, her voice sounding guarded and wary as she sat.

"Are you kidding? You were a legend. Helped put Coldwater Cove on the map with all the records you set. You and Chase Sanders were the talk of the town. I was and still am a big fan." Rory sat back down.

"Thank you." She looked uncomfortable. "But I meant remember me from the investigation."

He schooled his features into compassion and sympathy. "Ah, your mother's accidental death. She was a good person. Did a lot for this town. It hasn't been the same without her."

"Well, I'm glad to hear you're on the pro-Elizabeth side. Not everyone was a fan of my mother being mayor."

"I remember that as well." He puckered his brow, trying to look sincere. "It's a shame some people are so close-minded. That's the problem with a small town, especially in Maine. People tend to be set in their ways and don't like change. So what brings you home? I'm assuming your father. I heard about his illness. My condolences."

She clenched her jaw. "He's not dead yet, Sheriff."

"I didn't mean it like that." *Well, hell.* He rubbed his temple. "I'm sorry. It's been a long day, but that's no excuse for insensitive behavior. I didn't think I would see you around this office again, considering how your family felt about our department." He paused, gauging the obvious tension in her features and feeling a need to reassure her. "Things are different now. I'm the new sheriff, so please, tell me how I can help you?"

She stared at him with determination blazing from her amber eyes. "You can re-open my mother's case."

He blinked. Of all the things she could ask for, that hadn't been one he'd considered. "Excuse me?"

"Yes, Sheriff, you heard me right. I'm not a little girl anymore, and my mother didn't die by accident." Stacy paused for a few seconds before finishing with, "She was murdered."

Rory's elbow slipped off his desk and he caught himself before falling off his chair. He chose his words carefully. Whatever the cost, he couldn't let this case be reopened. "I realize losing your mother must have been terribly hard, Stacy, but her death was ruled an accidental drowning. A tragedy. I can assure you the case was thoroughly investigated before being closed. I can't just reopen it."

"You can, and you will."

"Now, listen—"

"No, *you* listen. It's Ms. Buchanan to you, Sheriff. I have a voice, and I won't stop talking until I've been heard. No one fought for my mother back then," she thrust her finger at him, "but you can damn well be sure that I will now."

He had to admire her courage and conviction and would love to be backing someone like her. This was exactly the kind of wrong he dreamed of setting right under his term in office, but sadly he had too much at risk. He masked the panic and forced sympathy into his tone. "I understand you're upset, but I'm afraid you won't get very far. I'm only trying to save you from more heartache."

"You let me worry about my heart." She nailed him with a hard gaze. "I'm afraid *you're* the one who's mistaken, Sheriff."

He narrowed his eyes, studying her in a whole new light. She wouldn't be as easily charmed as he'd thought. "How so?"

"Because I have proof."

His stomach pitched and he nearly lost it. "P-Proof?" He cleared his throat. How much did she know?

In lieu of speaking, she pulled out an old battered shoe and just stared at him. "Recognize this?"

It took him a moment, but then his eyes widened. "Where did you find that?"

"Mariner's Marina."

He resisted the urge to wipe the beads of sweat from his brow and tried to sound professional. "And how did that happen?"

She pulled out a folded up note and handed it to him. He schooled his features as he took the note with a steady hand and read it. He felt his Adam's apple bob as he swallowed hard. "Your mother was found in the cove weeks after she went missing." He donned a pensive expression before saying with authority, "This doesn't prove anything."

"This was dated the day she went missing," she replied with conviction. "She must have met someone at the marina, and they killed her."

"Look, it's my job to poke holes in your theory. She still could have fallen in by accident."

"I would expect nothing less from you, Sheriff, and honestly, that was my first thought." She paused a beat. "Until I checked. I highly doubt she tied an anchor around her ankle and threw herself off the dock by *accident*."

"What are you talking about?"

"Just beyond the drop-off, there's an old anchor with a rope tied around it. It has a loop at the end about the size of someone's ankle, and my mother's stocking is still caught in the knot. It was too heavy for me to lift. If you check, you will see what I'm talking about."

He sat there stunned, his mind scrambling for a way out of what was becoming an impossible situation.

Stacy clearly struggled to fight off her emotions as she blinked back tears. "My mother was murdered, Sheriff. Thrown off the dock while still alive, left alone to drown in the cold, dark sea. I want her case re-opened and the murderer brought to justice so she can rest in peace, and my father and I can finally get on with our lives. I don't think that's too much to ask for, do you?"

"This is a lot to process," Rory said sincerely. He wanted to be a good cop and do right, but re-opening this case could ruin everything. "Are you sure you want to open old wounds and bring all this heartache and tragedy back to the forefront? What about your father's health? What about your mother's reputation. I seem to remember that being in question. Maybe it's best to let it all die with her."

"So much for being on my mother's side," Stacy spat. "You say you're different than your predecessor. Prove it. Do your job, Sheriff." She surged to her feet. "Or I'll find someone who will." Leaving the evidence on his desk, she turned around and marched out of his office, pausing in the doorway. "Just so you know, I made copies and took pictures, documenting everything I saw. I'm a journalist. I know what I'm doing and so will the whole world if this somehow disappears." And then she was gone.

Rory's day had started filled with hope and a sense of purpose. Now he stared at the glaring evidence before him filled with anxiety and a sense of defeat. He had no choice. He had to reopen Elizabeth Buchanan's case and investigate it as a murder even though it meant he might lose everything. But that didn't mean he would go down without a fight.

He buzzed his secretary.

"Yes, Sheriff Evans?"

"Roberta, clear my schedule for today. I have a pressing matter I have to attend to that can't wait."

"Sure thing. Anything I can help with?"

A humorless laugh slipped out in the form of a sarcastic chuckle. "Unfortunately no, this is something I have to deal with myself." He hung up, knowing he might be too far gone to help, but there was one person he was going to see, because he sure as hell wasn't going to take the fall alone.

* * *

"No, no, no..." I sat in my car parked beneath the shadow of a large maple tree down the street from the sheriff's office, my worst fear unfolding.

Stacy Buchanan stormed out of the building, climbed into her small Prius and pulled away from the curb. Easing out of the shadows, I followed at a safe distance behind her. She was supposed to be in town because of her father's health. Last I heard, the man could still function fairly well on his own. So what else was she up to?

And why the hell was she at the sheriff's office?

Elizabeth Buchanan's death was ruled an accident. I had gotten lucky. Her body was never meant to be found. I'd nearly had a heart attack when she'd floated into the cove a couple weeks later, just when I had started to relax. The warm temps and salt water had covered any signs of foul play, but I still hadn't breathed easy until the FBI pulled out and the case was closed.

Back then, the only thorn in my side had been that special agent who wouldn't let the case go, but luck had been on my side when the agent was forced into early retirement. I had taken it as one more sign my actions were justified, same as I would be justified in what I had to do now. She was older. Smarter. Maybe she knew something none of them did. I had no clue what it could be, but I couldn't risk her dredging up the past.

I followed her, biding my time until I figured out where she was going. She surprised me when she turned off the main road and headed to the outskirts of town instead of her house. My pulse skittered into overdrive when she pulled into a park, climbed out of her car, and disappeared onto the path.

Coldwater Cove was known for its gorgeous parks through rich woods that opened into brilliant meadows filled with wildflowers. This particular park was an old remote one with a rarely used jogging trail winding through the woods and ending along a clearing at the top of a rocky cliff. A cliff overlooking the ocean. By-passing the parking lot, I drove my car a little further up and onto an old gravel road that bisected the path. Putting it in park, I slipped on a pair of gloves and climbed out of my car.

I had gotten lucky again.

* * *

STACY WALKED along the old jogging trail she used to run in her youth when she was conditioning for her long distance swim meets. Oh what she would give to return to those simpler days when all she had to worry about was winning. Being a grown up sometimes wasn't all it was cracked up to be. She was only twenty-seven, but she felt ancient. Trying to get her father settled, dealing with her childhood home, and seeking justice for her mother was all too much. She felt the weight of the world crushing down on her. Swiping a tear from her cheek, she took several deep breaths to try to control her anger.

Sheriff Rory Evans.

She clenched her jaw. The man was a piece of work. She remembered him well. She used to have the biggest crush on him, so handsome and charming and mysterious. She'd always liked older guys. Maybe because boys her own age had seemed so immature, especially after her mother had died and Stacy had been forced to grow up in a hurry. Evans had flirted with her even back then, but then again, he'd pretty much flirted with everyone.

Apparently nothing had changed.

He'd obviously charmed his way to the top, and now he honestly thought charming her would be so easy. She shook her head. She wasn't as naïve these days. She saw him for exactly what he was. A coward. He hadn't wanted to go against the town in the past by fighting for her mother, and it was clear he didn't want to now, either. Well, Stacy was determined to get to the truth, with or without him.

But first, she needed to pull herself together. She couldn't go home this upset. Her father would know something was wrong. He might have been her rock before, but she needed to be his now. There was no way he could handle the truth in his current state. It would kill him. Not about to lose both her parents, she took in the world around her and let the hometown she could no longer deny still loving soothe her.

Her feet scuffed along the worn dirt path as she walked. She kicked the occasional pine cone out of the way, ruffling the pine needle carpet. Rays of sunlight streamed through the branches, flickering as the breeze blew through the trees, creating a breathtaking light-show. A large bird's wings flapped as it soared through the treetops, while squirrels and chipmunks scrambled about the forest floor. She paused for a moment and smiled as a fawn followed its mother, somehow instinctively knowing it was safe. Hunting season was over. A twig snapped behind her, sending chills up her spine.

Or was it.

This wasn't the first time she'd felt eyes on her since she'd been back. She whipped around but didn't see anything. This was Maine, after all. Could it be a hungry bear? She'd been away too long. First she made careless mistakes in the water, and now she should have known to bring bear spray. She stood ramrod still and listened for several moments. Nothing but normal sounds of nature greeted her, and she let out a sigh of relief. Her active imagination and thoughts of her mother's murder were obviously playing tricks on her brain.

Turning back around, she kept walking. The ocean was calling to her as it always did. She could hear the waves cresting and lapping against the rocky shoreline down below. She was close to the end of the trail now. Another sound snapped behind her. She shot a look over her shoulder, and this time she saw a shape dart behind a tree.

A human shape.

She wasn't crazy and the shape wasn't just in her imagination. She was being followed. Hunted. The sudden realization that her mother's killer could still be in town and Stacy could be in serious danger hit her hard. The murder had happened during tourist season, and it was tourist season again, and she was back in town. Trying not to freak out, Stacy realized while she might be older, she was still an athlete. Turning around, she sprinted into action and ran as fast as she could toward the ocean. She kept peeking over her shoulder, but she couldn't make out who was following her. They did a good job of staying just off the path behind the shadow of the trees, but they were still there. She could feel their presence, hunting her like prey.

She ran harder which wasn't easy in a silk blouse, a pencil skirt, and strappy flat sandals. She'd wanted to look grown up and be taken seriously so she'd worn her work attire. A lot of good that had done. She'd come straight from the sheriff's office, not thinking about what she was wearing and wanting to clear her head. She also had only intended on going for a walk, but now that she was running, the strap on one of her sandals broke and her shoe slipped off. Sharp twigs, pebbles, and acorns cut her foot. Wincing in pain, she hiked her skirt higher ripping the seam, but she kept running.

The sounds behind her were getting closer. She started sobbing, so many emotions surging through her: sadness, anger, panic, fear, regret. She didn't want to die. She still had so much to live for. At last she broke through the clearing and fell straight into the fence that ran along the edge of the cliff. She sucked in a sharp breath as it splintered down the middle and gave way. Letting out a scream for all she was worth, she tumbled over the edge with a section of the fence clenched tightly in her hands.

Her grip was strong and fierce as she came to a jarring stop, clinging to the wooden slat with one hand as she dangled over the edge. She'd scraped her legs when she bounced off the sharp rocky side. Her ears rang with the sound of her heartbeat thundering through her drums. She couldn't catch her breath. Thoughts of her father whispered through her mind, and she held onto that as she slowly grabbed the fence with her other hand and started to climb. Her muscular swimmer's arms and shoulders were the only reason she could pull her tall frame up with just her bare hands. That and the surge of adrenaline rushing through her.

She made it to the edge when the fence she held started coming loose from its anchor in the ground.

Fear surged through her once more. It was true what they said. Her entire life seemed to flash before her eyes in an instant. Hot tears leaked out and ran down her cheeks and she closed her eyes, not wanting to witness the end. She accepted her fate and tried to make peace with it as the fence came loose completely, and she started to fall to her death. This was it. At least she would be with her mother again.

A strong hand grabbed her wrist in the nick of time to save her...or maybe to finish her off, she suddenly realized. Her eyes flew open and her lips parted as she looked up into the face of the person who had chased her through the woods. Shock rippled through her core.

Trent Clark.

The question was: was that good or bad?

6

TRENT WAS A BIG GUY—TALL and strong—but so was Stacy Buchanan. She didn't have an ounce of fat on her, which posed a problem. Muscle weighed twice as much as fat. He wasn't complaining. She looked amazing. Super skinny was not attractive in his book. A woman who could take care of herself was a huge turn-on for him, but at the moment it made saving her that much more difficult.

With his pulse thundering in his ears, it took every ounce of his strength to pull her up over the cliff's ledge. He was terrified he was going to lose her. When her feet cleared the edge, he fell back, pulling her on top of him, afraid to let go. Every inch of her was plastered to the length of him, reassuring him she was alive, she was breathing, she was going to be okay. He'd gotten to her in time, but what about next time?

"I can't breathe," she wheezed, her face buried in his chest, and he loosened his arms from the bear hug hold he had on her so she could roll off of him and gasp for breath.

He sat up and looked down at her, struggling to catch his own breath. "Jesus, you scared the hell out of me," he finally got out. Her wild curly auburn hair had fallen halfway out of its fancy bun, her face was streaked with dirt and tears, her clothes ripped, and her skin scraped and smudged with blood.

"Y-You chased me." She stared at him with a mixture of confusion and fear.

"What are you talking about? I run this trail at least three times a week. I like it because usually I am alone. I didn't think anyone used this trail anymore." His gaze ran over her, and he raised a brow. "And certainly not dressed like that."

"I used to run this trail when I lived here a long time ago. I went for a walk. Needed to clear my head before going home to my father." She sat up gingerly and reached for her face, wincing as she touched a bump on her forehead. "So let me get this straight. You mean to tell me that wasn't you behind me on the path?"

"I was ahead of you, almost to my truck in the upper parking lot at the end of the trail when I heard someone scream. I came running back to find you dangling over the edge. Scared me half to death." He scrubbed a hand over the top of his buzz cut. "Now I'm the one who needs clarification. Someone was chasing you?" He looked around but didn't see anything other than a few forest creatures, trees, grass and birds. "Who and why?"

She seemed to startle at that, as if just remembering she could still be in danger, her eyes darting around and looking scared. "Yes, I was definitely being chased. As for who, I have no clue. As for why? I'm guessing it has something to do with the evidence I found. At first I thought it was an animal, but then I saw a human form dart across the path into the shadows. I couldn't tell who it was because it happened so fast, but it was definitely a person. And they obviously didn't want to be seen because they stayed off the path, but I heard every stomp of their feet." She squeezed her eyes shut.

"Do you know what it's like to be hunted, Trent?" Her voice shook. "That's what if felt like."

He reached out slowly, trying not to startle her, but he couldn't help himself. She looked so damned vulnerable and afraid and beautiful, he admitted. He cupped her cheek and ran his thumb beneath her eye to wipe away a fresh tear.

"It's okay, Stacy. I'm here, and I'm not going to let anything happen to you, today or any day that I'm still in town. Got it?"

She opened her eyes and looked deep into his, her desperation to feel safe as clear as day. It was plain to see she needed that, needed him, and it felt good. Too damn good considering his mission.

"How are you going to protect me?" she finally asked. "That must be some training they gave you at WPS."

She was trying to make light of the situation, probably so she wouldn't freak out over what had just happened to her. She had no clue he had been through far worse while he'd served in the military and on this mission since then.

"I was in the Marines, remember? I've got your back, Buchanan." He matched her lighthearted tone, but then let his voice turn serious. "I'm here for you. I hope you know you can count on me."

She pressed her lips together as if to stop the trembling over his sincere words, because they *were* sincere. He meant every single one. "That's a first for me. Someone I can count on. I haven't been able to count on anyone other than my father in a very long time," her jaw hardened as she added, "especially not the police."

"I take it you took your evidence to Sheriff Evans, and it didn't go so well?"

Fresh tears sprang loose, and she nodded.

Trent didn't say anything, just looked at her. Damn she was one hell of a woman. He took her in his arms. She stiffened at first, but when he pulled her onto his lap, she let him. She cried into his t-shirt and let him rub her back and comfort her. It felt good to hold someone close again. And not just anyone, but her. She felt so right in his arms, her body pressed warm and snug against his. No words were necessary, he just wanted to be there for her.

She sat there for a while until her breathing regulated and her sobs subsided to sniffles, and then she pulled back enough to look him in the eye. "I feel so stupid. I have no clue why I'm crying like a baby. If the sheriff doesn't want to help me, I'll figure this thing out on my own. Nothing new for me. I'm used to being alone."

"You're not alone, Stacy, and you're hardly a baby. You were hunted down like prey and nearly died yet you kept it together and held on, trying to save yourself. And you almost did. I only helped a little." Trent brushed her cheek with his fingertips. "You're the real hero."

"I'm just glad you were there." She grabbed his hand and held on tight. "Thank you. I don't know what I would have done if you weren't."

"I know what I would have done." He turned his hand over and linked his fingers with hers. "I would have been the one crying like a baby, and I'm not afraid to admit it."

She eyed him with surprise and curiosity. "But you hardly know me."

His gaze bore into hers. "I know enough."

Her lips tipped up at the corners ever so slightly and her cheeks flushed pink, but her tears had dried up and she no longer looked terrified. Mission accomplished.

"You ready to get out of here?" He let go of her hand and smiled tenderly.

"God yes."

"That's what I thought." He chuckled as he stood up and reached out a hand to help her to her feet.

She straightened and let out a cry when she stepped down on her bare foot. "Wow that hurt more than I thought it would."

He frowned and leaned down to look at the bottom of her foot—the one with the missing shoe. It was covered with deep cuts that probably needed a stitch or two. "There's no way you can walk out of here on that."

"Well, I'm certainly not staying." She laughed harshly, looking around a little warily again.

Before she could protest, he lifted her into his arms and started walking.

"Trent, you can't carry me all the way to your car." She wrapped her arms securely around his neck. "I'm too heavy."

"Nonsense. You're tall, not heavy, especially cradled in my arms." He kept walking. "Besides, my truck isn't that far."

"Where are we going?"

"To the hospital, and then to the police station. We're going to report what happened to you. If that doesn't get Sheriff Evans to reopen your mother's case, then I don't know what will. But I do know we won't stop until we have some answers."

* * *

"OH, GOD, ELIZABETH, NO!"

Mack rushed into the exam room at St. Joseph's Hospital. He hated hospitals—white lab coats, needles, the smell of antiseptic. All of it screamed illness and death to him. He'd never been able to cling to the possibility of hope and life, not after all the life that had been taken from him long ago. He was shaking all over. He couldn't lose his Elizabeth again. She lay on the exam table, looking so vulnerable.

Suddenly she sat up and tilted her head to the side. "Dad? It's me, Stacy." A thin line creased her forehead and worry filled her amber eyes.

Mack stood to his full height of six-foot seven, but that didn't stop him from feeling ancient. And confused, he reluctantly admitted. He let out a heavy sigh and his shoulders slumped as a persistent ache formed in his temples.

"Sir, are you okay?" A big man in the corner drew Mack's attention. He wore athletic shorts and a tank top as if he'd been working out, but they were covered in dried dirt and blood. He looked oddly familiar with his dark haired military style buzz cut and hazel eyes.

Mack sat down in a chair and tried to concentrate. Suddenly the word *Dad* registered, and everything came back to him. His daughter Stacy sat on the exam table, and the muscular man in the corner was Trent Clark, the man who delivered his medicine each month. Relief surged through Mack that his memories came back, but a bone-chilling fear hit him hard when he acknowledged they wouldn't always. His stomach twisted into knots of pain and sadness.

How much longer did he have before he lost them all?

"Dad, you're scaring me," Stacy said.

Mack took a breath and stood back up then walked over to her. "I'm here now, sweetheart. No need to be afraid." His eyes widened when they took in her ripped clothes, cuts, scrapes and bruises. "My God, what in the world happened to you?" A surge of panic seized him. He touched her face then ran his hands over her arms and legs, finally taking her hands in his own. "Are you okay?"

"Dr. Hurn said I'm fine, just a little beat up and bruised."

"You left this morning but didn't say where you were going. I thought maybe to a job interview with the way you were dressed all fancy."

Her eyes darted to Trent's and an unspoken message passed between them. "Dad, there's something I need to tell you before it comes out and you hear it elsewhere."

"Do I need to sit back down?" he joked, but the way she looked at him took the humor right out of his comment. He sat on the edge of her bed and squared his shoulders. "Okay, shoot."

She told him everything that had happened from the beginning. Trent might be out of the military, but Mack knew that didn't mean he had stopped protecting and serving. He had silently moved from his post in the corner to a strategic position behind Mack in case he fell over, which wasn't at all out of the realm of possibilities with the way Mack was feeling right now. He was glad Stacy had a man like Trent to help her. He was decent and loyal and strong. Glad they both did because something told him they would soon need all the support they could get.

"Dad, say something, please." Her words broke through his fog.

"You should have come to me first."

"I didn't want to upset you. I wasn't even sure I had enough evidence to prove anything. I went to see Special Agent West first because he was the only one who was on our side back then, but he's too far gone to be of any help. Lost at the end of a bottle with no fight left to give."

"I didn't know you went to Boston," Trent said, sounding surprised.

Stacy shrugged. "How'd you know I went to Boston?" She looked at him in confusion and with a little bit of suspicion if Mack wasn't mistaken. His head was spinning as he tried to keep up with everything that had transpired. "I only said I went to see the special agent who had been in charge of my mother's case back then," his daughter continued.

Trent lifted his hands in an innocent gesture. "It's a small town. When I first moved here, I heard the rumors. And then, when I got to know your father, I did some reading about the case. I remember reading West had been forced into early retirement and that he'd relocated to Boston, ordered not to step foot back in Coldwater Cove. That's a shame about what happened to him. He sounded like he was a good guy."

Stacy seemed to relax a little. "He was, and I do feel bad for him, but he had the chance to help me right the wrongs now. As far as I'm concerned, he's a coward, just like every other cop I've met. They're either corrupt or cowards, unwilling to get involved. So I'm simply going to solve this case on my own."

"Like I said before, you're not alone. I think I've proven that already. I will help you as much as I can with fixing up your house and looking into your mother's murder when I'm not working on my other job, if you'll let me."

She stared hard at him but then seemed to make up her mind about something as she nodded slowly. "Okay. I'm smart enough to know I can't do this alone."

"Wait, I'm still trying to process all this." Mack's mind wasn't as sharp as it used to be, but it was still there nonetheless. "I just don't understand who would want to kill your mother? It hurts to know I failed her for so many years by letting her killer walk free." He studied his only child, who looked so much like her mother. "But make no mistake, I will not lose you, too. I wouldn't survive that, Stac. Someone tried to kill you today, and they would have if it wasn't for Trent. Now, I don't much like cops either, but Sheriff Evans will re-open this case if I have anything to say about it. He won't have a choice with the evidence that's before him. You need to let him do his job. He's not Pratt. Promise me you will stay out of this. I mean it. Promise me...*please.*"

She stared at him for a long moment and finally nodded her agreement, but Mack knew his daughter well. She was a competitor, a fighter, always had been. She got that from him. She wouldn't stop looking into her mother's murder until there were no more questions and justice had been served. Same with him. He knew she would worry herself sick if she knew he planned to do a little investigating of his own. So he wouldn't tell her. He would work out a few details with is lawyer, but he was pretty sure he could swing what he had in mind. Coldwater Cove was full of secrets. What would be the harm in one more? Besides...

He had a plan.

* * *

"I'm telling you right now, Mayor, I'm not going down alone." Rory stood in Thomas Zuckerman's office with the door closed and the shades pulled shut, while his assistant Soo Young Lee held down the fort.

When Thomas had taken over for Elizabeth Buchanan, he'd fired all of her staff except for Soo. Rory couldn't blame him. Everyone knew Soo was going places. A rising star the new mayor would have been foolish to let go. Now in her thirties, the past ten years had proven exactly that. She was destined to be the next mayor when Zuckerman retired. It didn't hurt his campaign that she was easy on the eyes, either. Normal office sounds clattered in the other room, no one the wiser that anything other than everyday political business was being conducted.

Do your job, Sheriff. Stacy's words haunted him. Didn't she know he was trying to do just that, but she was fucking it all up.

"Calm down, Sheriff. No one is going anywhere." The mayor broke through Rory's thoughts. In his mid-fifties, he still colored his hair black, kept it gelled and parted on the side in a distinguished fashion like a greasy politician. He'd greased many palms to get to where he was, all right, and had worked closely with Pratt.

"Elizabeth Buchanan beat you fair and square back then. She might have shocked half the town, but the other half supported her in a big way. I have no choice but to reopen her case with the evidence that has come forward, especially now that her daughter was stalked today out in the woods. When this town hears Elizabeth was murdered, there will be plenty of people who might think you did it so you could be mayor."

"That's crazy," the mayor said, trying to appear unaffected, but Rory could see the fear lurking behind his steel-gray eyes.

"No crazier than half the shady things that had been going on back then."

Zuckerman's eyes cut to Rory's. "Who's to say they're not still going on now?"

Rory ground his teeth. "Not for long now that I'm sheriff."

"Don't forget how that came about, boy." An evil smirk twisted the mayor's lips. "You have as much blood on your hands as I do."

"That's the point." Rory narrowed his eyes to slits.

"We can't let that information leak. We've both got a lot to lose."

"Agreed." The mayor stared right back, his smirk fading quickly with the reality of the situation they were in. "How do you intend to stop it?"

"Me? Try we. The same as we always have. Get rid of prying eyes."

A heavy pause filled the space between them.

"Then you know what you have to do." Resignation and acceptance settled over the mayor's face.

"Agreed, as do you." Rory might be forced to reopen this case, but that didn't mean he couldn't steer the investigation the way he wanted it. Elizabeth had enough enemies. He just needed to find one who looked guilty enough and make it stick.

Case closed.

7

MACK WATCHED his twenty-eight foot fiberglass fishing boat slowly make its way back into the harbor after a long day's lobster haul just off shore. Some of the smaller fishing boats had a single engine because they primarily fished close in to shore, but his girl had two. She had a standing shelter with a low trunk cabin, open cockpit, and sloping rails from bow to stern. Hauling in traps was much easier with a shorter distance from the water to the rail in the back of the boat. He'd upgraded his ancient boat for this beauty a few years back because she was equipped with a hydraulic trap hauler, CB radio, depth sounder, and radar. Everything he'd ever need for productive trapping and fishing charters.

Then he'd had to go and lose his mind and ruin it all.

He sighed. He was a fifth generation lobsterman and the end of the Buchanan line. Stacy hadn't wanted anything to do with fishing, so he'd had no choice but to sell his boat to one of his stern men, named Roy, who had graduated from the apprenticeship program and had a full lobster license now with trap permits of his own. His other stern man's name was Wally. A funny character and a good worker, but he was nowhere near ready to be a captain.

Mack missed it. Fishing was in his blood. There was nothing like heading out at eight in the morning with the wind in his face. Spotting a black and white buoy dancing across choppy waves was a rush. His muscles twitched with the memory of using the gaff to catch the line with the hook then grab the rope with both hands while leaning back and pulling with all his might until the hydraulic trap hauler took over and hoisted the forty pound metal contraption out of the water. Pulling in two to three hundred traps a day was physically demanding, but he'd loved every minute of it.

The excitement he used to feel over seeing a trap full of red lobsters, as he hefted the cage he'd built and repaired many times with his own hands over the starboard railing, flooded back to him. He'd had one hell of a crew. They'd worked together seamlessly without him having to say a word. His two stern men would jump into action, with his more experienced man, Roy, sorting the lobsters according to size and banding the claws with rubber bands, while Wally would fill the bait bag with herring and reset the trap.

Mack had felt such pride in being at the helm, reading the digital screens, considering the current and the layout of the ocean floor, and determining where the best spots were to drop the traps overboard. Navigating the ocean took skill, gave his life purpose. Elizabeth had been so smart—first a teacher and then mayor —while all he had been able to do was fish.

After he'd lost his Beth, and Stacy had moved away, fishing was literally all he'd had left, but now he was about to lose that as well. Men like him didn't retire. He'd always assumed his golden years would be a time of reflecting on and reliving his glory days with people who knew their worth: Stacy, future grandchildren, fishermen young and old. He supposed he would lose his memories of his friends and family, too. But there was nothing he could do about the cards he'd been dealt, and he wasn't here to reminisce.

He was here to get some answers.

Roy docked *The Queen* to have his haul weighed and inspected. The harbormaster and Coast Guard were present as well. Mack waved to Charlie Wentworth and noted he didn't look very good these days, but then who was he to talk. He smiled to himself as he glanced back at his old girl. Fishing boats were often named after a woman. Roy had kept the name out of respect to Mack and his tribute to his sweet Elizabeth, and Mack appreciated that more than the man could possibly know.

Truth be told Mack missed his crew almost as much as his boat. Roy still had Wally, who was now the senior stern man, and it looked as though Roy had hired a new man Mack had never met instead of one of the locals. The sailor had thinning red hair with a scraggly red beard. He looked a bit on the old side to be a new crew member. He had to be in his sixties. Standing six feet, he looked to have a physique that had once probably been impressive but was now weakening with age. Not exactly the kind of guy Mack would have pictured Roy hiring.

And Wally was Wally—sandy blond curls, a beer gut, and a sunny disposition. You could always count on him to cheer you up when you were down, given the competitive nature of their trade. Some captains got luckier than others. They all shared a bond, but tensions could arise and tempers often flared over the catch of the day because it wasn't just a sport to them. It was a dangerous, back-breaking means to feed their families.

"Hey, Mack, it's good to see you." Sincerity rang

through in Roy's tone as he peeled off his gloves and jumped down on the dock, still wearing his bibs and boots. His bald head gleamed in the setting sun, his black goatee was neatly trimmed, and the earring in his left ear sparkled defiantly as he strode toward Mack. Roy was loyal to a fault and you could always count on him to have your back.

Wally and the new guy took over with turning in the haul as Roy spoke, "How's retirement treating you, old man?"

"Old man is right. I feel ancient these days, but I'm hanging in there." Mack shrugged as they walked to a more private spot.

It had been a beautiful sunny day. The marina was still bustling with tourists who were returning from boat tours, deep sea fishing, and whale watching, while others were headed out on dinner and sunset cruises as gulls soared overhead, searching for scraps.

"I'd rather be out there with you boys still," Mack admitted. "Looks like you came in with quite a haul."

"That's the problem." Roy's expression registered his concern. "The lobster are almost becoming too plentiful. It's causing the price to drop, and it's getting harder to find people who want to go into this line of work."

"I can see that." Mack nodded toward the new guy. "He's not from around these parts, is he?" The man had on a pair of sunglasses, but something seemed oddly familiar about him. As if Mack had met him before.

"A buddy of mine who lives on Long Island told me about him. Asked me for a favor by hiring him and, well, I didn't have anyone else, so I figured why not give the guy a shot. He's not too bad." Roy squinted at his men as they worked, studying them, making sure they were doing everything right. Mack had taught him well. He would make a good captain for a long time to come. "His name's Kurt," Roy went on. "He gets tired a little too quickly but seems to know his way around a fishing boat, so for now it works."

"Well, that's good."

"Yup." Roy eyed Mack with a curious gaze. "Care to tell me what you're really doing here, Captain? Never known you to be much for small talk."

The corner of Mack's lip tipped up. "You know me well, Skipper."

It felt good talking like they used to, but he didn't have time to banter. He was on a mission. He glanced around the harbor. It was nearly dark now and the crowds were finally thinning out as people headed away from the marina.

"I'm sure you've heard by now that Elizabeth's case has been reopened and is being investigated as a murder." Mack's eyes met Roy's.

Roy's grin slipped and he nodded, looking somber now. "I'm sorry about that. It must be hard for a man like you."

Mack was a big guy who was steadfast and dependable. Everyone liked him, but they also knew he fiercely protected what was his. To cross him was not something anyone did on purpose.

"Like I said, you know me well." Mack clenched his jaw for a moment before continuing. "You also know my health is fading quickly."

Sadness and genuine pain crept into Roy's eyes. "There has to be something someone can do. Maybe—"

Mack held up his hand and skirted his gaze. He hated for anyone to pity him and, it was even worse to know people would mourn him. "It's okay, Roy. I've had a good life. I have no regrets." His thick gray brows drew together. "Or at least I didn't." He locked gazes with Roy so there would be no mistaking his words. "I can't go to my death without finding out who killed my queen, but I can't do it alone. I need your help."

"Done," Roy said immediately, without having a clue what Mack was going to ask of him. That was just the kind of man he was, and it filled Mack's heart with pride and warmth. He was like the son he'd never had.

Still, he had to ask. "Even if it involves turning on one of our own?" Sailors were like cops or military men in that they protected their own at all costs.

Roy's eye twitched and he hesitated a moment, but that was his only reaction. Standing a bit straighter, he said, "My loyalty is and always has been to you, Cap. I'm in, no matter the cost. I can handle myself."

"I have no doubts about that." Mack nodded his thanks. "You know I hate guns, and the whole town knows that Elizabeth was anti-guns. Half the folks didn't like it when she enforced stricter gun control laws. Everything she did was always about the kids. To keep them safe and give them the most advantages she possibly could to help them succeed, even if it meant angering certain people. I know you're an avid hunter yourself."

Roy nodded slowly. "But I never had anything against Elizabeth or her enforcement of stricter gun control laws. Guns don't kill people, but not every *person* should own one."

"I know that, Roy, but I also know that not everyone felt the way you did back then or now. What I need from you is to think hard and try to remember who might have hated Elizabeth and what she was doing to their town, as mayor, enough to want to harm her. I remember hearing there were a few sailors who had a grudge against her, but none of them would ever say so in front of me. I would never have put you in this situation back then because I knew my wife being mayor came with complications, and I thought she had died by accident. But now that I know she was murdered, that changes things."

77

"I understand." Roy squinted, looking pensive. "Give me some time, let me do some digging, and I'll get back to you."

"I appreciate it, Roy."

"I know, Cap." He reached out and squeezed Mack's shoulder. "Don't worry. We'll find the bastard responsible, and he *will* get what's coming to him. You can damn well be sure of that." With a fierce expression in his eyes and a determined gait, Roy strode back toward his boat but bypassed his crew and headed straight toward a group of captains.

For the first time in a while, Mack suddenly didn't feel so alone.

* * *

THE NEXT MORNING Stacy stood just outside the back door to her house as she talked to her father's lawyer, Louis Vito. He stood only five-foot-five and had a belly nearly as wide, but he had the thickest salt and pepper hair in town. His pride and joy, perfectly trimmed and styled with plenty of products. Stacy hadn't seen him in years, but her dad trusted him implicitly. She was the executor of her father's will and had power of attorney to help him make decisions now, as he needed it, and later, when he no longer could.

"Am I making the right decision, Lou?" Stacy rolled her head on her neck, trying to ease the tension she felt in selling her father's house and pushing him into the assisted living complex when he was making it more and more apparent every day that he didn't want to go.

"It's not my place to say, Stacy." Lou had been her family's attorney since forever, and she had known him all her life. "As a friend of the family and, off the record, I can honestly say I see him changing a little more each day. It breaks my heart to see him leave this house he loves so much, but he's getting more forgetful and confused. I just don't see how he can manage the upkeep of a home by himself, let alone remember to take his meds and make his doctor's appointments. I really don't see what other choice you have."

She did have a choice. She could move in with him, but now that she knew her mother was murdered, it would be even harder to be happy here. Not to mention her dreams of a future with ESPN would be lost forever. Her father would never have let her give that up if he had known about the offer, yet the man was too stubborn to move away with her. He needed her help, end of story.

She sighed deeply and pinched the bridge of her nose. "Are you sure he can afford the repairs we're doing?"

"You know your father. He never spends a dime on himself. Never has. He made good money as a lobsterman back in the day and other than spending money on you, he socked most of his earnings away. That's one area I can ease your worries about."

"Thanks, Lou." He said all the things she wanted to hear, yet something seemed a little off. Like he'd maybe left something she didn't want to hear unsaid. Then again, she found herself questioning everything these days, so it was probably just her.

"Anytime." He winked, tipped his head, and then headed off to his car, stopping to talk to Gary Sanders on the way.

When they finished talking, Gary continued down the path to join Stacy. "The place is really coming along nicely. Mr. Clark is doing a fine job. If I didn't double-check the address, I would barely recognize the place."

"Trent has been amazing. The people he called were fair and honest and did a great job outside. Come on in and take a look at the progress he's made inside. I think you'll be pleasantly surprised." Stacy limped on her stitched foot, that was wrapped and encased in a boot, as she led the way into her kitchen and dining room with Gary following close behind. They'd wanted her to use crutches for a week, but she'd refused. A boot was fine and gave her more freedom, even if it did sting and pinch with every step. She came to a stop by Trent.

"Mr. Clark, I have to say I'm impressed. Your craft is very skilled, and you don't seem like a stranger to physical labor," Gary said. "I somehow see you in this line of work more as a package carrier, no disrespect."

"None taken. Please, call me Trent, and thank you. I enjoy working with my hands and creating things. It gives me satisfaction, but working for WPS pays the bills. I was a former Marine so, yes, you can say I'm used to hard work."

"Ah, that must be it, then. And hey, if you ever want to do this full time, I have a ton of clients I could recommend. Your craftsmanship is exceptional."

"I'll keep that in mind if I decide to stay in Coldwater Cove. I tend to move around quite a bit. It keeps me from getting bored."

Trent's gaze locked with Stacy's, and she felt the heat of her blush stain her cheeks. He'd come to her rescue twice and had been so gentle and supportive and kind, comforting her when she'd been vulnerable and had needed it most. He knew she wasn't staying in town permanently and obviously neither was he. Getting involved would be pointless, but there was no denying the chemistry between them was growing.

Her father walked downstairs at that moment and gave Gary and Trent a funny look. "Stacy, would you like to introduce me to your guests? It's a school day. You know your mother wouldn't like you having company before your swim meet."

Gary's smile slipped and a look of concern swept over Trent's face while Stacy's heart ached.

"Dad?" she said gently, drawing his attention away from the men. "Did you take your medicine this morning?"

Her father met her gaze with a look of confusion. "Medicine. Right." He headed into the kitchen and opened a couple of bottles, then swallowed the pills with some water as he stared out the window for several minutes. Still within earshot, none of them said a word. They didn't dare so much as move. A few moments later, her father turned around, and his eyes widened in surprise.

"Gary, what are you doing here? It's good to see you, my friend."

Gary's shoulders relaxed, and he smiled. "Why, I came to see you, buddy. You ready to talk a little more about Whispering Pines?"

"Not really, but I will." Mack led the way out onto the front porch to give them privacy but not before Stacy had seen the concern on his face.

Her father might be trying to hide the fact that even he was worried, but she knew he was. He could tell when he had a moment of confusion, and her heart broke every time she saw his shame and embarrassment. Being the kind of father he was, he always tried to hide his feelings and make light of his episodes, but she knew better.

It was slowly killing him on the inside.

"You okay?" Trent asked from behind her.

She took a deep breath and shook her head. "No. This is going to be much harder than I thought, and it's only the beginning." She brushed away a tear. "I hate seeing him this way. He's always been my hero. Big, strong, safe. How am I supposed to be his?"

Trent wrapped his arms around her in a hug, and

she let him. Spinning around she buried her face into his chest and hugged him back until the lump in her throat subsided. He didn't say a word, just held her tight until she felt better. She stepped back out of his embrace but threaded her fingers through his as she looked into his beautiful hazel eyes and knew she was in trouble. Smart idea or not, she didn't have the strength to stop whatever was happening between them. She needed him too much.

"Thank you," she whispered and then cleared her throat. "I really don't know what I would do without you."

He stared at her lips as if he wanted to kiss her but didn't dare. His Adam's apple bobbed once before he replied, "Ditto." He squeezed her hands once and then let go as if he were fighting the same battle. "So now that we've made some progress on the house and your father's busy with Gary, how about we take a break in the kitchen and go over your mother's case."

"You took the words right out of my mouth," she said on a breath of relief as she led the way into the kitchen before she did something stupid.

8

LATER THAT DAY Stacy headed into the County Clerk's office where the Town Council held their meetings. Trent was going to talk to a guy he made deliveries to who was a member of the school board while Stacy talked to the County Clerk. She wore shorts and a t-shirt, having just finished working on her father's house. This far north in Maine could still be cool, but July was shaping up to be a beautiful month. Her mother had always loved summers in New England, though she never did get much time off. It wouldn't have mattered anyway, with Stacy's father fishing non-stop and Stacy swimming, family vacations were unheard of.

As mayor, Stacy's mother was pulled in several directions. She was responsible for many decisions that affected Coldwater Cove. The revenue the town generated had to be dispersed to various programs. Part of her job was to decide what percentage would go to which program: money for new construction, upkeep of roads, safety enforcement, educational programs, and more. No matter which program she favored more heavily, there would always be someone who was unhappy with her decisions.

Elizabeth had strongly favored educational programs the most, followed closely by safety issues. The
school board had been divided when more money went
toward athletic programs than music and art programs
such as band and theatre. The town council had been
divided when more money went toward stricter enforcement and harsher punishments for violators of
gun control laws and gambling than new construction
and upkeep of the roads.

Dissention among the departments she worked
with came with the job. She'd known that, as well as the
risk she was taking, but had someone been so upset
that they would go as far as blackmail and murder to
get what they wanted? Stacy still didn't understand
what her mother could possibly have done worthy of
blackmail, and was admittedly a little afraid to find out.
But no matter what it turned out to be, her mother
hadn't deserved to die. Stacy wouldn't rest until she
found out why someone thought she had.

Slipping her Prius into the only parking spot left,
she realized just how much she loathed rental cars.
With the tourist season in full swing, big oversized
SUV's were in abundance, as most people traveled in
packs when on vacation. Even with a small economical
car like hers, parking in the cramped parking lot full of
people was not an easy task. Cracking the door open a
hair, she peeked out. There was no way to squeeze her
body through the opening without scratching the mon-
strosity next to her. Left with no choice, she rolled
down the window and proceeded to climb out, earning
herself several odd stares from pedestrians milling
about and a few scowls from the locals.

Her tall height and curly auburn hair made her
easily recognizable. Initially people had welcomed her
back with a warm sympathetic reception, but now that
she'd had her mother's case reopened as a murder in-

vestigation, she'd received many cold shoulders. The regulars didn't want their town's reputation tainted in any way, especially during tourist season. With an awkward wave to the room, Stacy ignored her flushed cheeks and raised her chin a notch as she walked with confidence into the building. She had just as much right to be in Coldwater Cove as anyone else, probably more-so.

The office was filled with people asking about the parks and rec programs, summer camps, and other various things to do around town. As well as local people lodging complaints or disputing town matters about everything from zoning laws to taxes. The chaos made Stacy's head spin.

"Stacy Buchanan, I was wondering when you were going to look me up. It sure took you long enough, girlfriend. Your father's not the only one who missed you, you know," came a familiar voice that brought an instant smile to Stacy's face.

"Laura Baker, you look fantastic." Stacy locked eyes on her childhood friend and made a beeline over to her desk to give her a big hug. "You're the County Clerk?"

"That I am." Laura grinned devilishly.

Laura was a little bitty thing, only five-foot-two with short blonde hair like tinker bell and lavender eyes. She'd been on the swim team with Stacy, and they'd been inseparable. Stacy was the star, but Laura didn't mind. She loved being a part of the team even though she knew she was too short to really compete. Her stride wasn't nearly as fast as those who had longer legs. She looked like a little gymnast still, with maybe a few more curves, but they suited her well. So did the big diamond wedding band on her hand.

"It's Laura Baker-Flemming now." She winked after noticing Stacy's gaze.

Stacy's eyes widened. "You married Tommy Flemming, the quarterback? I thought you hated Tommy. You used to call him a big dumb jock, and he called you a floppy fish."

"You know what they say about love and hate: they're practically the same thing. The big meathead still drives me crazy, but I honestly don't know what I would have done without him." Her smile faded a bit. "I was pretty lost when you left town."

Stacy squeezed her hand. "I'm sorry."

"I know, and it's okay. Tommy has been amazing. We've been married for eight years now, and we have five-year-old twin girls, can you believe it?" Laura handed her a framed picture from her desk of two girls in bathing suits at a swimming pool, reminding Stacy of Laura and herself when they were little. They'd met in kindergarten and started swimming together that very year. Stacy had avoided social media since her mother's death, not wanting to be reminded of anything or anyone from her hometown. She never should have let so much time and distance come between them.

"They're beautiful." Stacy ran her thumb over the glass, a little sad she'd missed so much of their lives already. "They look just like you, but with their dad's height."

"I know, right?" Laura beamed with pride. "I'm so excited. I have hope they'll be just as good as you were with those long limbs of theirs. I'm not trying to make you feel guilty, or anything. I'm just being honest. They've filled the little piece of my heart that emptied after you left." Her gaze met Stacy's with sincerity and genuine happiness. "I'm just so glad you're back."

"Me too, but it's only temporary," Stacy said gently. "I plan on leaving at the end of summer."

"Well, we'd better get started then." Laura glanced around assessing the office for a moment, then stood up and placed a sign on her desk that said: On break, back in fifteen minutes. "Everyone's taken care of by other staff members for the moment and my assistant can hold down the fort for a bit if anyone else comes in and needs help from me. Come on, we've got some catching up to do, sister."

Stacy laughed, feeling like she'd stepped back in time as she followed her best friend to a secret hiding place like they had done when they were kids. In this case the break room would have to suffice.

Once they were seated on a comfy couch with a cup of coffee, Laura studied her with concern. "How are you doing, really? I heard about your dad, and your mom's case being reopened as a murder investigation. Someone chased you on the old jogging trail? I know you're a superstar, but that's a lot to handle, my friend."

Stacy closed her eyes for a moment and swallowed the lump in her throat. She'd never had a sibling and her mother had been gone for so long. Laura was the closest thing to a sister she'd ever had. It had been hard staying away from her, but Stacy hadn't been ready. Every time Stacy so much as even thought about Laura, the pain and memories of what they had both gone through came rushing back.

"It's hard, but I'm okay." Stacy took a sip of her coffee but could barely swallow the contents. "I really am so sorry, Laura. I never should have shut you out. Here you are worried about me, even after everything I did to you." Stacy's eyes welled up, and immediately so did Laura's. "You reminded me so much of my mom. She'd always been like a mother to you after your mother died when you were little. When I lost her, I knew that you did too. You needed me back then and I let you down. I truly am so happy you found Tommy. I owe him." Stacy chuckled. "Wow, *that* is something I never thought I would hear myself say."

Laura laughed softly as she wiped her eyes. "He will *love* hearing that. Seriously, though, thank you for apologizing. It means a lot, but we both got through it and became awesome. Not that we weren't always, but we're both happy now, right?"

Stacy shrugged, and immediately thought of Trent. She couldn't help but be a little envious of Laura. She and Tommy were obviously so in love and had a darling family to prove it, everything Stacy had thought she'd never wanted. Until Trent had come along and made her start to yearn for too many things.

Not ready to deal with those feelings, much less talk about them, she said, "I got a job offer from ESPN."

A beaming expression burst over Laura's pixie face, and she clapped her hands. "Oh my God, that's fantastic!"

Stacy smiled, realizing just how much she had missed this. "It was, but I couldn't take it." She kicked off her flip flops and curled her bare legs beneath her, pulling her t-shirt down over her shorts and crossing her arms over her middle.

"Why? Are you crazy? Obviously that's not what you wanted to do. Just look at your body language." Laura shook her head in bafflement. "I've followed you and kept up with you through your dad. Isn't ESPN everything you've ever worked for?"

Stacy nodded, feeling regret weigh heavily on her shoulders. "It is, but I can't let my dad down."

Understanding and sympathy dawned in Laura's pale purple eyes. "He doesn't know, does he?"

"No, and he can't find out. He would never let me turn down the offer. I tried to get him to move in with me, but he won't, and there's no way he can live alone in our house for much longer. I can't leave until I know he's being taken care of, yet he's so unhappy over the thought of moving. It's all just one big mess. And then there's my mother. To think that someone murdered her is just awful. She was alive when the killer threw her into the ocean like garbage. I won't stop looking until we find out who did it."

"I think that's what everyone's afraid of." Laura set her empty coffee cup down and leaned forward.

"What do you mean?" Stacy set her cold coffee beside Laura's, having been too worked up to take more than one sip.

Laura looked toward the open break room door to make sure no one was standing there before responding. "I've heard gossip around town. Whispers about secrets being revealed and cover-ups."

Stacy's heart started beating faster. "From who?"

"You know gossip, it spreads like wildfire. Who knows what's true or not or even who the original source was? All I know is I've heard things repeated in this very office, and Tommy has heard buzz around his shop. He's a car salesman so he deals with locals as well as tourists renting cars."

This could be the lead they had been looking for. "Can you tell me what the secrets and cover-ups are in reference to?"

Laura's face revealed her helplessness. "The mayor's office, the sheriff's department, the youth program for starters."

"Wait, I'm confused. Then or now?"

"That's the million dollar question, isn't it? It's so frustrating. Unfortunately, I don't know any more details than that, but I can promise you you're not the only one who won't rest until Mama Beth's murder is solved. I owe her that much for everything she was to me and did for me. Someone's gotta pay."

"Agreed. The question is, who?"

Stacy left the County Clerk building and walked back to her car. The big SUV that had been parked beside her was gone so she wouldn't have to climb through the window again, she noted with relief. At least one thing had gone in her favor. She started to open her door when a piece of paper beneath her windshield wiper caught her attention.

"What on earth...?" She grabbed the paper with a sinking feeling. Sure enough it was a ticket for parking in a handicapped spot. She frowned and glanced up to notice a handicapped sign she could have sworn hadn't been there before. Looking back at the note, there was something written at the bottom.

JUST DOING MY JOB.

SHE HEARD A CAR START, so she looked out at the street and set her jaw, her shoulders tensing immediately. Sheriff Rory Evans pulled away from the curb and sent her a wave as he drove away.

So much for things going her way.

* * *

TOO FUCKING CLOSE.

Stacy Buchanan was getting too fucking close to figuring out the truth, and I couldn't have that. After her mother had slipped free from the anchor and floated into the cove, I should have figured out how she'd gotten there right then. I should have gone back to that dive of a marina and retraced my steps, but I hadn't. At the time I'd wanted to stay far away from that marina so no one could connect me to it. They'd come a long way with DNA and shit, and I hadn't wanted to take the chance of being connected to the scene of the crime no matter how careful I had been.

And when her death had been ruled an accident, I had thought I was in the clear. I'd stayed under the radar.

To think my undoing might all come down to a fucking shoe.

I shouldn't have left anything to chance. I never imagined her shoe and stocking would still be down there after all these years. I would have thought nature and currents would have taken care of any left-over evidence. I should have double-checked. The real truth was I had been afraid. I wasn't a great swimmer myself. Elizabeth had been half dead when I had found her. In fact I'd thought she *was* dead. All I had been doing was trying to protect what was mine by getting ridding of the evidence. No one could fault me for that.

I had tied the old anchor around her ankle. When I realized she wasn't dead, I'd had a moment of panic and had second-guessed myself. I hadn't set out to kill someone that day, but when the opportunity presented itself, it had been the answer to all of my problems. Besides, I hadn't really killed her. I'd pushed her into the water and had let nature do the rest. It hadn't been as hard as I had thought. I'd justified that I wasn't the one to really kill her. Nature was. And it was all her fault because of what she had done.

She'd had it coming.

I was a good person, I told myself for the millionth time. In the end I paid the ultimate price anyway. I hadn't done anything like that since, and she'd left me with no choice that night. At least she hadn't suffered; she'd been unconscious. I couldn't say that for her daughter. Stacy was going to suffer, and I was going to look forward to it. She needed to atone for the stress and anxiety she was causing me now. Unlike her mother, she had been fully aware I was chasing her through the woods. I didn't like scaring people, but history was repeating itself. Once again she was leaving me with no choice. I was still protecting what was mine. That was my job. And just like before, nature had nearly done my dirty work for me.

If only the fence had fully given way, she would have fallen to her death without my having to lay a hand on her. But this time that pain in the ass delivery man had saved her. Someone was always showing up at the worst time. First her father and now Trent Clark. How many people would I have to get rid of to keep my secret safe? I didn't like to get my hands dirty, but I would if I had to.

Keeping my distance, I waited out of sight in the rental car I'd switched to, then pulledaway from the curb and followed Stacy's Prius as it finally passed by me. The weather was holding, and the traffic thinning. I'd gotten lucky before with her not seeing me when I'd followed at a distance, but I couldn't afford to get sloppy. I'd needed a rental car for what I had in mind today. By the time I was done with her, she wouldn't have a clue what hit her, literally, and, hopefully, then my troubles would be over with once and for all.

Stacy drove through town and headed toward the outskirts where her father's house was, just like I suspected she would. She hadn't ventured far or stayed away from him for too long since she'd been home. The traffic thinned even more as we headed up the coast toward the water. The back roads were lined with trees, the roads narrowing.

Perfect.

It was now or never. Gathering courage I stomped on the gas pedal, and my car surged forward, slamming into the back of her Prius before she knew what happened. Everything happened so fast, yet it seemed as if my world was spinning in slow motion. I watched through her rear-view-mirror the look of shock followed by fear that filled her eyes as she tried to regain control of her car to no avail. It spun wildly out of control in a three-sixty and then rolled over into a ditch, slamming into a tree.

I blinked, and the world righted itself to normal speed. My heart thundered in my chest as I pulled over and cut the engine. Was I really capable of running someone off the road? Had I really just done that? She could be dead right now. It had been so long since I'd actually killed someone. Did I really have it in me to do it again? I swallowed hard, accepting that the deed had already been done. There was no going back now.

She hadn't seen me.

Smoke rose above her car and a hissing noise sounded, but that was the only noise I heard when I stepped out of my car and walked toward hers. Glancing over my shoulder, my rental car's bumper wasn't even scratched. Slipping on my gloves, I resigned himself to my fate. It was time I took matters into my own hands and finished what I had started once and for all.

9

TRENT NAVIGATED the back roads in his truck on his way to his rental cottage after not getting anywhere with the school board. He hadn't lived in this town long enough to form friendships strong enough for citizens of Coldwater Cove to betray their own. The people he knew were merely friendly acquaintances. They might be all for spreading gossip within their close-knit circles, but not so much to outsiders.

He planned to shower and change and then maybe swing over to Stacy's house to see if she had any more luck with the town council. Who was he kidding? That wasn't the only reason he planned to visit her. He couldn't get her off his mind. The sparks were flying between them, and he hadn't even kissed her yet, but that didn't mean he hadn't thought about it often.

Yet?

Jesus he was in more trouble than he thought. He couldn't afford to get involved with anyone, let alone *her.* It was too risky. She didn't know everything about him, and if she ever found out, she would lose all trust in him. Dammit, why did this have to be so hard? It was tearing him up inside. His sense of duty had him protecting his own, but what about him? What about *his* happiness? Stacy Buchanan was everything he never even knew he was looking for: smart, funny, sassy, and sexy as hell.

She kept him on his toes, that was for sure. She was too damned stubborn for her own good and not about to listen to reason from anyone. When she had her mind set on doing something, there was no stopping her. He was finding out in a hurry not to argue with her. It was pointless. Instead, he made sure he kept tabs on her to keep her safe, which wasn't easy. The woman had taken at least ten years off his life so far, and he was afraid she was just getting started.

"What the hell?"

Rounding a bend in the road, Trent had to swerve to avoid an SUV parked halfway in the street. He pulled his truck off to the side just beyond the vehicle and then jogged back to see what had happened. Stopping in surprise, he stared at the familiar man before him.

"Mr. Vito?" Mack Buchanan's lawyer? "Is everything okay?" Trent asked with concern. "I didn't recognize your car."

"It's a rental. Mine's in the shop." Louis wrung his hands together. "I'm fine, but I'm not so sure about everyone else. I was on my way to Mack's house to discuss some changes he wants incorporated in his will when I came across the accident."

"Accident?" Trent just now tuned into what the old man was talking about. He peered down into the ditch at the overturned car, and his stomach bottomed out. Only one person in town had a car like that. "Stacy!" he shouted as he scrambled down the ditch to the driver's side door of the Prius, sending a flock of birds bolting toward the sky. Steam billowed out of the engine with a hiss.

Fear seized him. She had to be okay, she just had to.

Clearing his throat he asked, "Stacy, can you hear me?" while assessing the situation.

His heart was hammering in his chest but his training had kicked in, forcing him to remain calm. She'd worn her seatbelt, thank God. Suspended upside down, her head had a scratch and a small bruise, but that was all he could see. The sun was sinking lower in the sky and the trees blocked what was left of the rays. He reached inside the car and felt for a pulse. A strong beat throbbed beneath his fingertip, and relief surged through him.

"Is she okay?" Louis asked from the road.

"I think so. She's just knocked out, I'm guessing."

"I'll go on ahead and talk to Mack to prepare him." Louis opened the door to his SUV, hollering behind him, "Want me to call an ambulance?"

"No, I've got her. I'll handle everything."

"Roger that." Louise shut the door and pulled away, kicking dirt up from beneath his tires.

Trent stroked Stacy's pale cheek. She looked so vulnerable, it tore him up inside. "Stacy, sweetheart, can you hear me?"

She blinked her eyes slowly open, and he could see panic start to set in.

"Easy, sweetheart, it's okay. I'm here. You've been in a car accident, but you're going to be all right. I didn't want to move you until I asked you a few questions." The terror left her eyes, and she relaxed a little. "Can you move your hands and feet?"

She tested them and nodded.

"Good. Does your stomach or back hurt?"

She moved a bit and then shook her head no. "Just a headache."

"Okay, I want you to feel for your seatbelt and unbuckle it. I won't let you fall."

Trent reached inside and supported her suspended

body while she did as he asked. When the belt released, he tightened his arms and caught her, gently pulling her through the window. Once he had her safely outside the car, he picked her up and carried her back to his truck, in case her car exploded, not saying a word until they were safe. Dropping the tailgate, he set her on it and then stood before her inspecting every inch of her. This feeling of terror and a need to keep her safe was so foreign to him.

"I'm okay," she said, shaking off her state of shock and sounding stronger by the minute. She pushed her wild curls off her forehead. "What happened?"

"No clue. I was on my way home and saw Mr. Vito standing in the road by his rental car." The words rental car had her eyes widening. "What is it?" he asked.

"I remember now. I left the county clerk's office and headed home. Suddenly I felt like I was being followed, but when I looked behind me all I saw was a rental car. An SUV. I couldn't see inside, but you know how it is around here during tourist season. Rental cars are all over the place, so I didn't think anything of it until it followed me to the outskirts of town. All of a sudden, it slammed into me from behind, and I lost control. Everything was spinning before the impact, and then my world went black until you woke me up."

Trent narrowed his eyes. "Do you think it could have been Mr. Vito?"

"Louis? No way." She started to shake her head, but then she grabbed her skull with her hand as she winced.

Trent cradled her face in his palms. He couldn't help himself, he hated to see her in pain. Her hand slid down to cover his and their eyes met for a long moment.

"You scared the shit out of me again," he finally said in barely more than a whisper. "Are you trying to kill me?"

"No," she answered in a quiet silky tone, "but I think someone might be trying to kill *me*." Her soft amber eyes searched his with such faith and trust and hope, it nearly did him in. "I'm scared, Trent."

"Don't be." He set his jaw. "I promise you I won't let anything happen to you." At least that promise he could keep. "It would destroy me." He let his eyes say everything his mind wouldn't let him speak.

"It would?" She blinked. "Why?"

"I think you know why. Right or wrong, smart or stupid, it doesn't matter. I'm falling hard for you, Stacy Buchanan." Trent lowered his mouth to hers, giving her time to move away, but she didn't. His lips pressed softly against hers, and he moaned, sparks exploding.

Stacy's hands caressed his cheeks for a moment before slipping around his neck and pulling him in close between her knees. Trent deepened the kiss and wrapped his arms around her. One hand stroked her back while the other slid up her spine to slip into her hair and cradle her scalp as he explored every inch of her mouth. She tasted like sunshine and honey, the aroma of wildflowers intoxicating his senses. Her legs were crossed behind his back and she pulled him in tighter.

God, she felt so damn good pressed tightly against him. He couldn't get enough of this woman, and it scared the hell out of him. His forehead hit her bump and she flinched, so he broke the kiss but didn't let go. They held each other, absorbing the impact of what had just happened. This was probably the dumbest thing he'd done in a long time. Maybe there was a way out.

"Just so you know," she said in a breathy voice with that warm, melted butter tone of hers, "I'm falling hard for you too, Trent Clark."

Well, hell.

* * *

"THANK YOU FOR STAYING WITH ME," Stacy said to Trent in the exam room of the hospital ER.

Trent had pulled back almost immediately after she'd said she was falling for him too, which made her both relieved and frustrated. She knew as well as he did that getting involved wasn't a good idea, yet there was no way he could deny how amazing that kiss was. Rough whiskers, firm lips, musky scent and the flavor of coffee had swarmed her senses with a heady sensation of passion and rugged man.

Stacy had kissed a few men in her life, but had never felt the way she did when kissing Trent. It was wonderful being held in his powerful arms, his muscles capable of crushing her yet he'd held her so tenderly. But now he was acting like it was nothing more than adrenaline and fear and being in the heat of the moment that had bonded them. Nothing more.

Bullshit.

He knew it was more, just like she did, but he was afraid. She could relate. That was why she hadn't called him out on it. It was easier to shrug the kiss off and go about their business as usual, striving for normal when she feared nothing would be normal again.

"You're welcome, Buchanan." He smiled tenderly, but there was tension in the set of his shoulders. "What are friends for, right?"

"Friends." She smiled back, but it didn't quite reach her eyes. "Right."

Doctor Olivia Hurn came walking into the room, studying the clipboard in her hands. She'd been their family doctor for all of Stacy's life. She'd been friends with her mother back in high school and later friends with her father after her parents married. After Stacy's mother had died, it was obvious Olivia's feelings for

Mack had grown into something more. The hint of sadness in her eyes indicated even she knew there had only ever been one woman for Mack, and after Elizabeth had died, so did a piece of his heart.

Dr. Hurn smiled a smile that lit up her sea-foam green eyes. "As much as I love seeing you my dear, I'd rather it not be under these circumstances." She wore her white hair in a short, sophisticated style, and her chic glasses with the fancy chain perched on the end of her cute nose only added to her charm. She was tall and slim and her lab coat was clean and starched. Stacy had always adored her.

"Agreed." Stacy smiled back.

"Everything looks fine, no concussion, just some cuts and bruises." The doctor looked concerned. "You're free to go, my dear, but heed my warning. This is becoming a dangerous game you're playing, I'm afraid. Your stitches have barely healed in your foot, and now this. I'm worried about you."

Stacy's father came flying into the exam room with a flushed face and slightly out of breath. "Are you all right? Anything broken? Who did this?"

"I'm fine, Dad." She hugged him. "Really. Just ask Dr. Hurn."

Mack blinked and looked up at Olivia. Her face flushed ever so slightly, but Stacy noticed. "How's my girl, Doc?"

"She's fine physically, but mentally, someone needs to give her a stern lecture." She nailed Stacy with a no-nonsense look.

"Oh, trust me, I'm on it." Her father set his jaw in a determined line.

"Good, and how are you doing, Mack?" Doc Hurn's gaze softened as she took in his features in more than just a doctorly way.

He shrugged. "Ah, I'm okay. It is what it is."

"Yes, it is, I'm afraid, but you know I'm here if you need anything at all." She rested a hand on his forearm.

He covered her hand and patted it twice. "I know, Liv. And thank you. Don't know what I'd do without you."

"Well, then." She pulled her hand away and stepped back, looking a little flustered. "I'll let you guys talk. I've instructed my nurses not to fill this room, so take as long as you need." With a little wave, she left the room looking as calm and cool and professional as when she'd entered.

Stacy's father watched the doctor leave with a mixture of sadness and regret tinting his eyes, but just as quickly he turned his firm gaze on his daughter, making good on his promise. "You gotta stop doing this to me, Stac. My heart can't take it." He sat in a chair by her bed with Trent still on the other side of her. It felt good being flanked by the two men she cared most about.

"Well, I certainly didn't do this on purpose. All I did was go see Laura and come straight home. I can't help if someone followed me and ran me off the road."

"Sure you can," her father said with frustration. "You can stay out of this case and let the sheriff do his job."

She snorted out a laugh over that one.

"I couldn't agree more, Mr. Buchanan." Sheriff Evans said from the doorway of her room. "May I?"

"By all means. I wouldn't dream of standing in the way of you *doing your job*." She glared at him, the ink barely dry on the ticket in her purse that he'd given her.

His smirk said it all. "I'm here to take your statement if you're up to it."

"Don't you have deputies for that?" she ground out the words.

Her father refused to meet Rory's eyes and Trent

didn't say a word, just observed the situation unfolding before him in an oddly intent way.

"This case is special. I told you I would do everything in my power to help put this case to rest." The sheriff flipped open a notebook and pulled a pen from his shirt pocket. "So tell me everything you remember."

Stacy sighed dramatically, hating to have to work with him, but even she knew she needed all the help she could get. She recounted everything she could remember, leaving no detail out.

"And what were you doing at the County Clerk's office before that?" Rory asked innocently enough, but something in his tone seemed off.

Having no choice, she said, "I saw Laura." Deciding to take a gamble, she told him everything Laura had told her about the gossip surrounding old town secrets and cover-ups. "What do you think it all means?"

He rubbed his clean-shaven jaw. "I'm not sure. A few allegations were thrown around when Sheriff Pratt was in office, but nothing was ever proven. I'm more interested in the allegations that surfaced when your mother was mayor."

"Now wait just a goddamned minute," Mack bellowed and surged to his feet, his fists balled.

Trent jumped up and stood between them. "Easy, Mack."

Sheriff Evans held up his hands in an innocent gesture, but the look in his eyes said otherwise as his gaze met Stacy's in a silent warning. "All I'm trying to do is find out who murdered Elizabeth Buchanan, your *mother*. Isn't that what you want? There had to be a reason someone wanted her dead."

"Yes I want my mother's murder solved but not at the expense of her reputation." Stacy stared him down with a warning of her own.

Mack reluctantly sat down, but Trent stayed by his

side. All the more reason to adore the man, even if it was against her better judgment.

"The FBI was in town for a reason back then," the sheriff said. "They were looking into something no one really knew about. My suspicion was the youth program. The program was your mother's pride and joy, and everyone knew she sank a good percent of the town's revenue into it. Caused enough enemies right there. The problem is the numbers didn't add up. The college recruiting events and scholarships and after school programs didn't take the amount of money being spent, but your mother died before anyone could prove what had happened to the rest of the money. Mayor Zuckerman took over and the FBI left. Ever since then the books have been fine."

"And most of the programs dropped," Stacy pointed out.

"Not all of them. There's still a scholarship event held in her name every summer. In fact, it's coming up soon. You should be proud."

"I am, but that's beside the point. What are you trying to say? You think my mother embezzled the money from the youth program back then? She would never do something like that, especially not if it affected the kids."

"People talk. Your father's an awfully private man. Lives by simple means, yet recently he's spending quite a bit of money on house repairs, and several charities have reported generous anonymous donations. I'm sure if I talked to Mr. Vito I would discover Mr. Buchanan's holdings are quite substantial." The sheriff looked her father in the eye. "So tell me, Mack. Where'd you get the money?"

"How dare you, you son of a bitch!" Mack's face turned crimson as he surged forward, but Trent held him back and whispered something in his ear.

"Just trying to do my job like you wanted, posing questions you will probably be asked as this investigation goes forward." Sheriff Evans pocketed his notebook and looked for all the world like an objective law enforcement professional just trying to get at the truth.

Stacy knew better. He was goading her father and pushing her, trying to bully them into admitting something or leaving it alone like the cops years ago had done. He had no idea how strong they both were.

"Good, Sheriff," she said firmly. "I expect nothing less from you."

"Maybe it's best if you left town for a while. Took a vacation with your father so you'll both be safe. I would hate to see anything more happen to your family."

"Oh, we're not going anywhere, Sheriff. The Buchanan's don't run from a fight, right Dad? We're stronger than you think, and we can take care of ourselves."

"You got that right." Mack gave Sheriff Evan's a look that would bring most men to their knees.

Rory tipped his hat. "Have it your way, but don't say you weren't warned. Looks like taking care of yourself hasn't paid off for you so far. I don't have enough manpower to keep you all safe and do my job."

"Don't you worry about that, Sheriff," Trent said in a calm, quiet, yet deadly tone which brooked no argument. "They have me."

Trent's gaze met Stacy's, and she suddenly knew that was enough. Whatever was between them, whatever they could give each other was okay. It was enough. They would take things one day at a time and worry about the rest later.

Right now they were a team.

10

BOB PULLED his hat low over his brow and kept his head down, trying to blend in as he walked along the pier of the Coldwater Cove marina. He loved the salty brine smell of the ocean, reminding him of when he was a kid. The squawk of gulls, the rumble of boat engines and the low horn of the ferry greeted him like an old friend. But he wasn't here to turn nostalgic. He was here to do a job. He'd been back for a couple of weeks, poking around to see what he could find out. It had been ten years since he'd worked Elizabeth Buchanan's murder case, yet it still felt like yesterday.

He'd felt like shit turning Stacy down when she asked him for help. She'd given him the lead he had waited so long for, but he'd let fear of failure stop him from putting this case to rest once and for all. He'd changed his mind almost immediately, but he hadn't told her. The less she knew the better, but damn it felt good feeling useful again. Like he had purpose, even though the powers that be would throw him in jail if they got wind of what he was up to.

Years ago he'd been on a task force looking into her mother's affairs. The mayor's office was under suspicion for missing funds from some of its programs, but her mother wasn't the only one under suspicion. Her father's fishing boat had been suspected of being involved in illegal activity, but the FBI hadn't been able to prove it.

Stacy said someone was blackmailing her mother. Maybe they had found out what had happened to the missing money that caused the discrepancies in the books and threatened to expose her. Or maybe her mother had been overlooking her father's illegal activities and someone threatened to expose that. Or, worse case scenario, her mother had found out about her father's illegal doings, and he killed her to keep her quiet.

Admittedly, that seemed crazy, but in his line of work, Bob had seen all sorts of things that didn't make sense and were hard to believe. Anything was possible. He had learned to be objective, keep an open mind and expect the worst. Bob would find out what really happened to Elizabeth for his own sake as well as Stacy's. He owed it to her, but she might get more than she bargained for. She would get closure, all right, but the question was....

Could she handle the truth?

There wasn't a cloud in the sky as the sun was setting over the harbor, the orange and red ball casting a fiery glow over the dark water with the promise of a beautiful day tomorrow. A fisherman's delight. Inhaling a deep breath, the smell of salt and fish and pine trees filled his senses. He loved the ocean and had grown up around boats before entering the FBI, leaving his brother behind to help their father in the shipbuilding business, but that didn't mean he didn't know everything there was to know about boats.

Vessels of various sizes were moored against the docks, hunkered down for the night. While the captain and crews were making their way into The Claw—a waterfront pub where all the regulars hung out. Bob had been there every night since he'd been back, but surprisingly he hadn't had a single drink. He thought abstinence would be more difficult. It turned out his drive to keep a clear head and solve this case outweighed his need to consume, giving him hope that he just might have the strength to beat his demons someday.

Bob continued walking toward The Claw. He'd heard talk around the docks about one of the fishing boat captains, named Barry Granger, having had a falling out with Mack Buchanan years ago. The man had also been a big gambler and hunter, which didn't make him a fan of Mack's wife either. Now that Elizabeth's case had been reopened and was being investigated as a murder, no one who'd known her back then was being overlooked.

Before Bob reached the door, Mack Buchanan himself made an appearance. Bob knelt down to tie his shoe until the big man disappeared inside. "Dammit," Bob muttered, not comfortable with getting too close to Stacy's father for fear of recognition.

Bob contemplated his next move when he saw a member of the Coast Guard head into the harbormaster's office. The act itself wasn't unusual, as a harbormaster often dealt with Coast Guard crews in keeping their waters safe. The fact that this was the third package Bob had seen the man deliver to Charlie Wentworth over the past couple weeks seemed suspicious. Something seemed off. Time to go to plan B. He veered to the right and headed toward the harbormaster's office.

Maybe the night wouldn't be a total waste after all.

* * *

MACK WALKED through the door of The Claw, and a feeling of nostalgia hit him hard. He used to frequent this pub years ago, when first starting out as a fisherman, and even later as a captain. But then he'd met Elizabeth, and his world had changed. He'd wanted to spend every second with her, and bars weren't really her scene. She was a teacher and later mayor, always concerned about her reputation being squeaky clean. That's why he'd never bought into the theory that she was involved in anything illegal. He'd known and loved her for over two decades and had finally been blessed with a daughter. That had been enough for Mack, and he'd never regretted it.

He admitted his distance had caused some issues with his crew back then. Barry Granger had worked for him since he could remember, but Barry was a wild one. He thought nothing of cheating on his wife, not to mention drinking and gambling away all of their money. When he wasn't fishing or boozing or at the track, he was at the rifle range with his buddies from the sheriff's office. Mack had overlooked a lot, but when Barry got drunk one night and made a pass at Elizabeth, Mack had drawn a line in the sand. They had come to blows, and Mack fired him. That had been the end of it.

Or so he'd thought.

He clenched his teeth over what Roy had found out for him. Barry had landed another job on board another boat but hadn't been able to let the matter go. After Elizabeth became mayor and enforced harsher punishments for illegal gambling and gun control violations, she'd alienated a lot of the folks in town. It had come as no surprise when she'd received a few anonymous threatening phone calls. She'd reported the matter to the sheriff's office and Pratt had promised to look into it, but nothing had come of it. When the calls stopped, she didn't feel the need to pursue the matter further, saying dissention came with the territory.

Allegedly, Barry Granger was the one who had made the calls.

Fury filled Mack. How dare the son-of-a-bitch harass his Queen Elizabeth? She hadn't deserved that kind of treatment while the slime ball had gone on to become a captain of his own boat. By God, if he was the one who had blackmailed her, Mack would do more than get him fired this time.

He would bury him and not think twice.

The Claw had been around forever and not much had changed, Mack noted. The inside was decorated with the same nautical theme it had sported for decades, with pictures of some of the biggest catches of the day throughout the years. The lighting was dim, the ambiance cozy, and classic rock hummed through the speakers while a reality fishing show played on the big screen TV hanging above the bar. The TV had been upgraded, as well as the lighting above the bar, but other than that, it felt like stepping back in time.

Mack peered through the crowd of fishermen, and just as he'd suspected, Barry sat at the end of the bar in his usual spot. Predictable as always, the man was a creature of habit. Mack made his way through the throng of people, nodding and making a comment or two along the way. He came to a stop in front of Barry, and Barry looked up at him in surprise.

"Now there's a face I didn't expect to see anytime soon." Barry grunted. He might be a creature of habit, but that was all that was the same. The years of drinking had taken their toll on him, leaving him with a beer gut, a puffy face, and bags beneath his dark brown eyes. He looked like shit, his milk chocolate skin waxy, the ladies' man he used to be all but gone.

"Get used to it," Mack responded in a low deadly grumble.

"Thought you were sick or something." Barry sipped his whiskey.

"Not sick enough not to be able to finish what I started." Mack paused a beat. "Let's just say I'm ready to right some wrongs."

"Missed me, did you? Are you here to grovel and admit you made a mistake all those years ago in getting rid of me?"

"Oh, I'm going to get rid of you, all right." Mack leaned closer. "But first I'm gonna make your life a living hell."

Barry's bravado wavered. "I was just messing with you. What the hell's your problem, old man?"

"You are. I might be older than you, but I'm bigger and meaner. You've known me long enough to know it's true. Besides, you look sicker than I do." He looked him over in disgust. The man smelled of stale smoke and sour sweat.

A look of wariness entered the younger man's dark eyes. "Ten years of nothing from you, and now this? Why?"

Mack took a long moment to stare at his former stern man until he began to squirm. Only then did he drop the bomb. Timing was everything in his line of work. "I know you were the one who made those anonymous phone calls to Elizabeth back then."

"Look, you and I had our differences in the past." Barry's nostrils flared as if he couldn't get enough air. "Everyone knew I wasn't a fan of your wife, but I'm not crazy, and I sure as hell don't have a death wish. I didn't kill her."

He held his hands up in an innocent gesture, but the fact that he didn't deny making the phone calls wasn't lost on Mack. Mack took a moment to study him.

Barry was a lot of things, but Mack didn't think he had it in him to kill anyone. He might be loud and obnoxious and a crappy husband and friend, but he was also a coward.

"Maybe you didn't kill her, but I'm betting you know who did." Mack slapped him on the shoulder as if they were long lost friends, his voice remaining low and calm.

"I swear on my wife's life I don't." Barry crossed his heart and Mack squeezed, pinching the sensitive skin between his neck and collar bone.

Mack gave him a sarcastic smirk. "Excuse me if I don't believe a word that comes out of that garbage can mouth of yours."

"Honest to God, I'm telling the truth," Barry whined, and Mack enjoyed every second of it. Barry might not have killed Elizabeth, but he deserved worse for the anxiety he'd put her through. "I wasn't the only one who had issues with your wife, no disrespect."

"Too late." Mack balled his fists, itching to punch him in the face. The only reason he didn't was because it would upset Stacy and Doc Hurn.

"I'm just saying the town was divided back then. And look, Thomas Zuckerman was all too happy to take her place as mayor. Maybe he had something to do with her death or someone who wanted him in office instead of her did it. Or what about all those kids? Your daughter and that Chase Sanders boy were stars. People do all sorts of things out of jealousy."

"Like blackmail?"

"What are you talking about?" Barry looked genuinely confused. It was clear he didn't know about the note. "All I'm saying is maybe you should be looking more closely at them instead of me."

"You let me worry about who I'm going to look more closely at, and let me know if you hear anything at all about my wife's murder. I know more than a few people who might care to look more closely at *you*. Funny how you always have money these days, when word around town is you never win your bets."

Barry paled but didn't say a word.

"We clear?"

The man clenched his jaw as if it killed him to say the words. "Clear as a fresh rain. I hear anything, I report to you, boss."

"That's what I like to hear." Mack slapped the man hard in the center of his back, letting the pressure of his hand linger in a silent message. After Barry's confirming nod, Mack left The Claw, feeling better already.

Don't you worry, my love, Mack mentally vowed. *I'm not going to stop until the bastard who killed you pays the ultimate price.*

* * *

SHERIFF EVANS STOOD in the shadows of a large boat on the dock of the marina, waiting for Barry Granger to meet him. An evening chill settled over the harbor like a bad omen from the sea. Sailors weren't the only ones who took signs seriously. The man was a loose cannon. Rory never would have chosen to work with him. In fact, he hadn't. That was all Sheriff Pratt's doing years ago, and once again, Rory was left cleaning up his former boss's mess. This shit was getting old real fast.

Granger had called him in a panic, asking to meet him on the docks. The man was always frantic about something, becoming more paranoid as he grew older. He came stumbling out of the bar, looking left and right in such an obvious way that if someone was watching him, they would clearly see his guilt rolling off him in waves.

"Pssst, over here," Rory said when Granger grew close.

"Where are you?" Barry said in a loud, slurred whisper.

"Exactly where you asked me to meet you," Rory hissed. "Jesus, man, pull yourself together. What the hell's wrong with you?"

Barry hustled over into the shadows, breathing heavy, the stench of stale whiskey turning Rory's stomach. Barry's eyes darted about like a madman. "It's over, man. Everything's falling apart. He knows something. He's going to find out, and he'll kill us all."

"Who are you talking about?"

"Buchanan," Barry spat. "He knows about the phone calls. I don't know how, but I think he knows everything." His eyes darted about once more, only this time they grew still and narrowed slightly. "Shit. I think I just figured out how he knows so much."

Rory followed Barry's gaze to see Captain Roy walk out of the pub followed by his crew of Wally and the new guy Kurt.

"Goddamned traitors betrayed one of their own." Barry started to pace, his boots scuffing the wood, the sound echoing off the water. He really wasn't very bright, Rory thought as he ground his teeth. Barry finally stilled before Rory had to make him, but Barry kept ranting on. "And for what? A former boss who doesn't give two shits about anyone except himself and his beloved Elizabeth? Bastards will get what's coming to them even if I have to take them out myself."

Rory was starting to think taking out Barry would ease his headache in a *big* way. He sighed deeply and pinched the bridge of his nose. "Okay, let me think."

"Well think quickly. Mack Buchanan wants answers and he wants them now." Barry blurted out the entire conversation he'd had with the giant of a fisherman, looking on the verge of a breakdown by the time he finished. "What are we going to do?"

Rory's temples throbbed. This case was giving him migraines and judging by the pain in his stomach, he was pretty sure he had an ulcer. "*You* aren't going to do anything." He thrust his finger in Barry's face and donned his best authoritative expression. "You've done enough damage by mentioning Mayor Zuckerman. No more gambling, no booze, no women. Go home to your wife for once and keep your fucking head down. I'll handle the rest. Buchanan has questions, so I'll give him some answers. I'm working on something. I should have a suspect soon."

"Who?"

"That's on a need-to-know basis, and you sure as hell don't need to know." Rory couldn't take the risk of Barry leaking crucial information to the wrong parties. The man was clearly unstable, and Rory was done with him. "All you need to know is that this case will be closed soon, but then we're through. Got it?"

Barry stilled, looking stricken, his face draining of color and turning pasty. "But Sheriff Pratt promised—"

"Haven't you heard? There's a new sheriff in town." Rory stared him down so there would be no mistaking his meaning. "I don't like you. Never have and never will. I didn't sign up for this mess, but you can be sure I'll finish it. And then I want you out of my town. It's time I started doing things *my* way around here."

11

STACY PULLED into the parking lot of Coldwater Cove Park, the biggest park in town. Laura had asked Stacy to be the guest of honor for the Elizabeth Buchanan Scholarship Foundation ceremony. For years her father had handled this honor on his own, never complaining when she made an excuse not to come home for it. The truth was she couldn't bear it. These scholarships had meant the world to her mother, and knowing she wouldn't be here to see them handed out was difficult. It was cowardly, and certainly not fair to her father, but she hadn't been strong enough to handle it. The ceremony reminded Stacy of all her mother had missed in her own life. Strong or not, she owed it to her father to be here now.

No more hiding.

The large gazebo that had been in the center of the park for as long as Stacy could remember had been beautifully decorated with summer wildflowers. Various picnic tables packed with people surrounded the gazebo on all sides, and the lawn that had been meticulously maintained was filled with lawn chairs and blankets. The smell of barbecue filled the air as laughter and the hum of conversation rumbled through the crowd. It warmed Stacy's heart to know that, for as many people who didn't like her mother as mayor, there were equally as many people who had adored her.

Taking a deep breath, she knew she couldn't wait any longer. It was time. She opened the car door to her rental and stepped out. Her Prius had been totaled in the accident, and since no one had been caught, she was dealing with the nightmare of her insurance company to work out the details of getting a new car. Of course her father had tried to buy her a new car, but she insisted she wanted to take care of the matter herself. Lately he'd been giving money to all sorts of charities and spending his savings at an alarming rate. It wasn't like him.

She'd questioned Louis about the change in his will, but the lawyer said his hands were tied. He was simply doing as her father bid him and as long as he still had his faculties, he was in charge of his own decisions. Louis had told her she would have to ask Mack for the details. When she asked her father, he was very vague in his response, reassuring her he had everything under control. Part of her wondered if he was going a little crazy from his Alzheimer meds. Dr. Hurn said she would follow up with him and for Stacy not to worry, but she could tell the doctor was as concerned as she was. Her father was up to something, she just had no clue as to what.

Walking through the throng of people, Stacy held her head high, her heart filling with pride as she joined her father and Laura by the gazebo. Her father wore his Sunday best, which for him was his newest pair of blue jeans ironed with a crease down the front, a button down shirt tucked inside, and a pair of boots. Her captain of the seas had never looked better. Laura was dressed smartly for success in her best suit, and Stacy had worn a skirt and blouse with her favorite leather sandals.

The entire town was there, as well as a few tourists who showed up to see what all the fuss was about. Mayor Zuckerman spoke into the microphone with authority, explaining who Elizabeth Buchanan was and all that she had done for the town, especially its young athletes. He said all the right things, but he had a politician's smile and mannerism. He always seemed phony, like he had some ulterior motive behind every action he took. Next, he introduced Stacy as the guest of honor.

Laura handed an envelope to Stacy and motioned for her to step up to the mic as the mayor stepped down to join his assistant, Soo Young Lee, as they networked the crowd. Laura and Stacy's father watched from the front row of the audience with Dr. Hurn close by her father's side. A large board sporting pictures of past recipients with Stacy and Chase Sanders at the very top was to the right of her.

Her gaze landed on Gary Sanders for a moment and caught him staring at the board with a look of pride, longing, and sadness all mixed into one, reminding her of her father and the way he sometimes stared off at the vast ocean like he was missing her mother and missing his life at sea. Gary blinked several times, as if fighting back tears, and smiled an embarrassed smile when he caught her studying him. Out of respect, she looked away only to meet Sheriff Evans' unreadable gaze. He tipped his hat in acknowledgement, and having no clue how to respond to that, she focused on the crowd instead of responding at all.

"Thank you everyone so much for coming here today. I know my mother would be thrilled, and it means more to my father than any of you can imagine." Mack beamed with pride as he wiped tears away from his

117

eyes. Stacy cleared the lump from her throat. "I know I haven't been around much over the past decade. It was hard for me coming back here. Something always felt off about how my mother died. As you all know by now I'm sure, my mother didn't die by accident." Stacy paused and let her gaze sweep over the crowd before finishing with, "She was murdered."

Sheriff Evans frowned in distaste no doubt for her giving voice to the elephant in the room. She hadn't set out to do that, but somehow it had just come out. The thought that the killer was still on the loose and trying like hell to shut her up fueled a fire in her to make sure they all knew she wouldn't be stopped. Hushed murmurs rumbled through the crowd as the wind kicked up in an eerie gust. She liked to think it was her mother cheering her on.

The organizers moved towards her, but she grabbed the microphone and stepped to the other side of the gazebo as she continued to speak. "Now that I'm back, you can rest assured I will find out what happened to her. For those of you who loved her as much as I did, I know you would want nothing less from me. For those of you who didn't, don't say you weren't warned. Sheriff Evans has assured me he is taking this matter very seriously and is doing his job. I'm sure he wants every one of you to feel safe again in Coldwater Cove, as do I."

Her gaze met the sheriff's once more. His remained unreadable, though there was obvious tension in the set of his shoulders and a muscle in his jaw bulged.

Stacy raised her chin a notch as she continued. "Coldwater Cove is a special place. My mother fought hard to keep her streets safe. She took pride in this town, and gave everything she had to ensure its youth had all the opportunities to succeed in life. That's why this scholarship is so important. Trust me when I say I will do anything to make sure her legacy lives on, and I will find a way to restore the Cove to its former glory."

Most of the audience clapped as she moved back to the podium and opened the envelope, while a few turned around and left.

"Congratulations to all of the deserving nominees. You should be proud of everything you have accomplished already, and I am sure you will go on to do great things. And now for the moment you've been waiting for." Stacy read the card before her. "And the winner is Emily Maynard from Coldwater Cove High School's swim team."

A tall girl with long black hair squealed in delight and clapped her hands, rushing forward to accept her award. "Thank you so much, Ms. Buchanan. I only hope I go on to become as big a success as you were."

"You're very welcome." Stacy smiled as Emily walked away. "And that concludes this year's ceremony," Stacy finished and then put the microphone back into its cradle.

She started to step down from the gazebo when a loud crack sounded. Looking up, she froze. It felt as if she had stepped outside of her body and floated above the scene, watching the events unfold below. A massive part of a big oak tree came crashing down. Her heart jumped into her throat. She was paralyzed with fear when suddenly something slammed into the side of her. Seconds before hitting the ground, she was turned sideways, her fall cushioned as she landed on a body. Air whooshed out of the chest beneath her, and she heard a grunt and wheeze. She blinked out of her daze of confusion and looked down into the face of her savior.

Trent Clark.

He always seemed to be there in the nick of time. It was uncanny and sometimes raised red flags to her, but she couldn't go there right now. He was the only one besides her father and Laura whom she truly trusted. She needed that trust, and someone strong to lean on. It suddenly hit her she was doing more than leaning on him. She was lying on top of him, and he wasn't breathing.

Scrambling off his chest, she rolled to her knees and ran her hands over his face. His eyes were closed. "Trent? Trent! Can you hear me?"

His face flinched in pain and finally he gasped for air, his eyes flying open in a wide dazed look. Relief surged through her. She'd only knocked the wind out of him.

"Oh, thank God. You scared me half to death." She didn't think, she just reacted by kissing him squarely on the mouth. Laura's eyes had filled with relief when she realized Stacy was okay, but now when Stacy looked up she saw them widen in surprise and curiosity over that kiss, which made Stacy frown just as quickly. Dammit, how did he make her forget herself and the world around her? "Don't do that again, you hear me?" She sat up and scooted back to put a little distance between them.

He raised a brow and the corner of his lip tipped up ever so slightly. "If you'd quit nearly dying, I wouldn't have to."

"Trust me, I'd like that just as much as you would."

He drew his brows together and sat up gingerly as he studied the scene unfolding around them. "What happened?"

She looked at all the people scrambling around the park in confused chaos, while the sheriff and his deputies tried to gain control of the situation. "I'm not sure. Part of that huge tree fell right where the podium was. We haven't had a storm in weeks. It shouldn't just fall like that, should it?"

He narrowed his eyes. "It might if it had help."

They both got to their feet as people still scurried about in a state of panic. Mayor Zuckerman and Soo Young Lee were trying to calm everyone down while Sheriff Evans and his deputies were inspecting the tree. Gary Sanders and Louis Vito were talking to Dr. Hurn who was listening to her father's heart.

Stacy's breath hitched, her own heart skipping a beat as she rushed to his side. "Dad, are you okay? What happened?"

Her father waved his hand at her and started to speak, but Dr. Hurn shushed him. "He's fine, just a racing heart," she finally answered for him as she put her stethoscope away. "It's not a heart attack, just anxiety. I'm ordering him to go home and rest, or I'll put him in the hospital myself." She gave him a stern look, and he was smart enough not to argue with her. "Gary, please take the stubborn mule home, and Louis, wait for me by my car. I'd like a word with you."

The men did her bidding, and Stacy's father didn't utter a protest, which was more than a little unsettling to Stacy. He must be worse off than she thought. She narrowed her eyes. Or up to no good.

Dr. Hurn gave Stacy a relieved yet disapproving look that cut her to the quick, making her feel selfish and like the worst daughter on the planet. "I know you mean well, honey, but this whole situation is getting out of hand. I want justice for Elizabeth as much as anyone. She was my best friend. But putting yourself in danger and losing your father in the process isn't worth it. It won't bring her back." Olivia squeezed Stacy's hand. "Now if you'll excuse me, I have a few pressing matters that need attending to."

"I know what you're thinking, Stacy," Trent said from beside her after she'd remained quiet for several minutes. His expressive hazel eyes softened with compassion. "It's not your fault. None of this is."

Stacy was shaking her head before he finished speaking, knowing she didn't deserve his compassion. "No, she's right. I am the one who started all of this. Suspicious things are only happening because I got my mother's case reopened. I never should have dredged up the past. Emily could have gotten hurt if the tree branch had fallen a few minutes earlier. Then there's my father and even you." Stacy stared into his eyes, letting her own fill with everything she felt but knew she couldn't say. "You're not Superman, you know. You're not made of steel. You *can* get hurt, and I'm not about to be the cause of it."

He rubbed her arms. "I'm fine, your father's fine, we're *all* fine. Your mother was murdered. That's not your fault either, and she deserves justice." He tipped her face up so she would look at him. His expression filled with tenderness and something she was afraid to identify. "Whoever is doing this is trying to scare you away from discovering the truth. You must be getting closer than you think."

"Not close enough." Stacy decided it was time to finish this. No more being afraid while waiting and worrying that something would happen. "I opened this can of worms, so there's no going back."

"We're in this together, remember?"

"I remember, and I thank God for you." She meant every word she said as she took his hands and pulled him down, softly pressing a kiss on his lips, deciding doubts or no doubts, she needed him. "I really don't know what I would do without you."

He leaned down and kissed her back for a long moment, making her every cell melt as he confirmed he was in this, too. Whatever *this* was. Then he added, "So what exactly does *no going back* mean?"

"It means we're done playing by his rules. We need to turn the tables on him now before anyone else gets hurt. What do you say we go catch ourselves a killer?"

"I say let's do this, Buchanan. You're stronger than you think. It's time this town found out just what you're made of."

* * *

GODDAMNIT! Did the woman have nine fucking lives?

I drove away from the park, gripping the steering wheel of my car as rage vibrated through me. It was getting impossible to kill her and make it look like an accident. She just kept digging and digging and asking questions around town. When she wasn't asking questions, her nosy father was. And Trent Clark was no parcel delivery man. He was too highly skilled for that. He knew too much about too many things and was always under foot. It was clear to see he had the hots for her, but there was more to it than that. He seemed too invested in solving this case.

The man had something to hide.

I, more than anyone, could recognize the signs. The question was what did he have to hide and why was this case so important to him? I was getting desperate. Obviously my plan of action wasn't working. Time to switch things up.

Time for plan B.

* * *

"THANKS FOR TAKING ME HOME, GARY," Mack said as he climbed out of Gary's luxury car and walked into the back door of his house, familiar smells of cookies and potpourri and Elizabeth inundating his senses.

Home.

There would never be any place that meant so much to him. There would never be any place where he felt closer to his Queen. There would never be any other place he would call home. Not like this. So there was really only one thing left that he could do.

Gary followed him inside. "It's my pleasure, Mack."

Mack sat at the kitchen table and Gary joined him. "You didn't have to walk me inside. I'm not *that* far gone yet."

Gary studied him with concern on his face. "No, but you did give us all quite a scare back there. Your face turned gray, buddy. I thought for sure you were having a heart attack. Frankly, you scared the shit out of me, pardon my French, but you and I have been through a lot together."

Mack grabbed a decanter of whiskey and two glasses. "Scared the shit out of myself, and I agree. We old bastards have been to hell and back. That's saying something." He handed the glass to Gary.

Gary didn't say a word even if the look on his face questioned if it was wise considering Mack's health issues.

Mack chuckled. "I know what you're thinking, but does it really matter? My days are numbered, my friend, and I want to remember the taste of a smooth, aged bourbon while I still can."

"I'll drink to that." Gary clinked his glass to Mack's and took a healthy sip.

Mack raised his glass again as a feeling of resignation settled deep into his bones. "I have something else we can drink to as well."

"Yeah, what's that?" Gary's brow furrowed as he complied.

Mack swirled the amber liquid as he stared down into his glass. "The house repairs are finished, and I've decided I want you to put her on the market."

Gary's eyes widened in surprise. "Yeah? I have to say I'm surprised but pleased. I think you're making a smart decision. The house looks great. I know I can get a good price for you." They clinked glasses and drank again. "Does this mean you're ready to commit to moving into Whispering Pines?"

"No." Mack didn't have to hesitate in responding to that question. He didn't want to move into Whispering Pines and had never intended on doing so. He'd simply kept the peace with his daughter by humoring her and going through the motions.

"Really?" Gary looked curious. "Do you have some place else in mind? Because I can help you with that. Just say the word."

"I have something else in mind, a better place that reminds me of my Elizabeth and the ocean, but I'm all set." Mack smiled at him reassuringly. He didn't need anyone poking around and asking questions before he was ready. His own daughter and doctor did enough of that. "I don't need any help, though I do appreciate all you've done for us."

Gary looked like he wanted to argue but sighed instead. "Like I said, it's my pleasure. And I know all about better places that remind us of our loved ones. Chase used to love the woods and running. That's why I bought a place on the outskirts of town. It makes me feel closer to him." His eyes filled with sadness and longing, and Mack could relate, but he couldn't afford to involve anyone else in his plan. "Well, I should probably hit the road, my friend." Gary stood and carried his glass to the sink. "You all set for the night? Do you need anything else before I leave?"

"Nope, I'm good." Mack poured another two fingers of whiskey into his own glass, not yet ready to face reality. "And I'd appreciate it if you wouldn't say anything to Stacy about Whispering Pines. I'll tell her when I'm ready."

"No problem." Gary shot him a wave and left quietly out the back door.

No, Mack wouldn't need Whispering Pines for what he had in mind. He was going to a better place than that. He might not want to face reality, but life had a mind of its own whether he was ready or not. He tossed back the rest of his whiskey and glanced at his watch. It was about time he put the rest of his plan into motion.

12

"HOW ARE YOU DOING OUT THERE?" Trent asked in a hushed whisper through his phone as he hid in his hiding place.

The sheriff had confirmed the tree branch that nearly fell on Stacy had been deliberately cut. He said he was looking into it, but Stacy didn't believe he was doing that any more than he was looking into her mother's case. Even after police divers had recovered the anchor with her mother's stocking attached to it just like Stacy had said, he still seemed to be downplaying the evidence. Stacy refused to sit idly by and let her mother's case grow cold again.

Crouching down, Trent sat behind a tree at Mariner's Marina, closely watching Stacy as he waited for her response. A hawk circled its prey over the nearby woods and an uneasy feeling settled over him. The sky was overcast with fat, gray storm clouds ready to burst open at any moment. A breeze kicked up off the ocean, the tide high with foamy crests on the peaks of the waves, the branches on the trees swaying wildly. It might be summer but the air had a definite chill to it, and a sense of foreboding permeated Trent's senses.

"As good as can be expected, I guess," Stacy replied

through her earpiece. She wore her wetsuit with her hair pulled back in a ponytail. She looked amazing even though seeing her dressed like that here brought back memories of her nearly dying in his arms.

Trent shook off his sense of doom, ignoring his gut and focusing on why they were here this time. Instead of waiting for the killer to attack when she least expected it, Stacy had decided to draw him out. After the scholarship ceremony, Trent had helped her spread the word in all the right places that a new lead had turned up at the scene of her mother's crime. It didn't take long for rumors to buzz throughout town.

Sheriff Evans had questioned Stacy, but she'd evaded him by saying the rumors were nothing more than that. And that if she'd had anything new to share with him, she certainly would. She wanted this case solved more than anyone. As expected, he hadn't bought it and had followed her around relentlessly. After finally shaking him, they'd doubled back, hoping the killer would think it safe to make an appearance.

Trent was a little nervous leaving her alone out there, but the way he figured it, he was close enough to get to her in time if she needed help. He knew enough to know that most killers had an MO. This one didn't use a gun or knife and he hadn't killed again that they knew of, so he probably wasn't a serial killer. Not to mention his attempts on Stacy so far had been in trying to cause an accident. He obviously didn't like to get his hands dirty.

Even with Elizabeth, he hadn't been able to kill her with his bare hands. He'd tied her up and thrown her into the ocean to let her drown. For whatever reason, he'd committed a crime of passion. And now that the case was reopened, he was obviously desperate to keep his secret safe. But was he desperate enough to reveal himself instead of striking from the shadows? So far no one had shown up.

"Don't worry, I'm right here," Trent said, needing to say or do something to reassure her. He felt helpless hiding in the bush, but he wasn't the one the killer wanted. She was. "You just let me know when you've had enough, and we'll call it a day."

"Let's give it a little longer." She glanced at the sky. "As long as the rain holds off, I'm good."

"Maybe pretend to be looking for something so you don't look suspicious."

"Good idea." She walked the length of each pier, looking around as if searching for something, like she had the first time.

Another thirty minutes went by. Finally, she started walking back to the car. Trent started making his way out from behind the tree when he saw her jump. Quickly crouching down, he pulled out his phone and took several pictures and remained silent. The plan was for her to press record on the device in her ear. He saw her touch her ear as she started talking to the big dark man who stood before her.

"Mr. Granger, you scared me," she said loud enough for Trent to hear, knowing he didn't have the best vantage point from where he hid.

"Long time no see." It was obvious, even from this distance, the man was checking Stacy out. "You've certainly grown up, little mermaid."

Stacy grimaced, and Trent clenched his fists and had to dig deep to remain professional. Something about this guy seemed slimy. Creepy even. And if Trent were honest with himself, he would admit he was a little jealous of *any* man looking at her that way.

"Funny how that happens." She crossed her arms over her middle. "I didn't expect to see anyone here. It's not exactly well known these days."

"I could say the same thing about you."

She shrugged. "Sometimes I come here to feel closer to my mother. My father used to bring me here to fish when I was little."

"You're not the only one. Mack was my mentor. Treated me like a son until he cast me aside for something better." Barry grunted, his face hardening. "Like Roy could ever be better than me. I made captain before he ever did. That right. There's proof I'm the better man. Got me a better place too."

"Have you been drinking? How did you get here? Do you need me to give you a ride home?" Stacy fired off her questions.

He stiffened. "None of your damn business. I'm fine, and I'm not going anywhere except fishing."

"In this weather?"

"Fishing's my excuse to my wife. I really come here to think."

"Oh, is something troubling you?"

"Yeah." He took a menacing step toward her. "You and the mess you caused by poking your nose in where it didn't belong." He thrust his finger into her shoulder, and she flinched, stumbling back a step.

"I found your hat, Stacy." Trent emerged from his hiding spot immediately, waving a Steeler's hat in the air to keep from punching the asshole in the mouth. He couldn't blow his cover now or everything she'd just put up with would have been for nothing. He feigned surprise. "Oh, I didn't realize we had company. I'm Trent Clark. I don't think we've met. And you are?" Trent asked as he joined her side, trying not to let his anger over the man daring to lay a hand on her show.

"Confused." Barry eyed him with suspicion. "I thought Stacy was alone." He looked at her with narrowed eyes. "Since when do you like the Steelers?"

"It's been ten years, Barry. A lot has changed about

me since then, but apparently not a lot has changed about you." She glared at him without backing down. "There's a reason why my father let you go. This is Barry Granger, Trent. He used to work for my father a long time ago, but he had a lot of problems, *drinking* being one of them," she ground out. "He had issues with my mother as well, if I remember right."

"Now wait just a minute." Barry backed away, his buzz apparently clearing in a hurry. "I see what you're doing. Don't you even be trying to link me to your mother's murder. I admit I didn't agree with her policies as mayor, but I sure as hell didn't kill her."

"Sounds like you had plenty of motive," Trent observed. "Her policies messed with your *problems*, I gather. Getting rid of her would have solved everything, not to mention a little payback to a man you once admired who cast you aside so easily."

"Who the hell are you?" Barry had a wild look in his eyes as he backed away further, his gaze darting between the two of them with uncertainty.

"A friend of the family." Trent took a step toward him, knowing with satisfaction just how intimidating he could be when he wanted to. And right now he desperately wanted to. "Where exactly were you the night Elizabeth Buchanan went missing?"

"With my wife. Ask her. She'll back me up." Barry sounded desperate.

"I'm sure she will," Stacy said, giving him a look of disdain as she stepped closer to Trent's side in a show of unity. "Everyone knows you bully her into saying exactly what you want."

"I think you're right. It's not good fishing weather, and I don't have to say anything more to either of you. If you have issues with me, you can speak to my lawyer." Barry turned and left in a hurry without looking back.

"Good idea, Barry," Stacy called after him. "I wouldn't say anything more, either. Trust me, you've said enough."

"That man's got problems, all right," Trent said to her when Barry Granger was gone. "Are you okay?"

"I'm fine. Barry is all bark no bite. He's guilty of a lot of things, but he's a coward. I don't think he's our man." She threw her hands up in the air and let out a heavy sigh. "I feel like we failed today."

"Not necessarily." Trent rubbed his jaw. "He might not be the killer, but there's no doubt in my mind he's hiding something."

Stacy's phone rang, and she checked the Caller ID. "Hi, Dr. Hurn. Is anything wrong?" Stacy's face drained of color. "We'll be right there."

* * *

"I CAN'T BELIEVE IT." Stacy stared down into her whiskey later that day as she sat at her kitchen table across from Trent. Wine was her drink of choice, but some things called for something stronger. "My father had a heart attack. A *real* heart attack this time. This is obviously too much for him, and it's all my fault. I should have been there for him instead of out playing cops and robbers." Her throat clogged up with emotion. She had to rehash what happened because it still didn't seem real.

"Your father is going to be fine." Trent's tone was gentle and full of reassurance as he sat beside her and took her hand. He was her rock, and he didn't even know it. "I know it was scary, but Dr. Hurn said his heart attack was mild. More of a wakeup call for him to slow down. He was the one who shouldn't have been out investigating by himself. This would have happened no matter what you had been doing."

She still couldn't believe her father. They'd never had secrets. Why now? "What was he thinking going to that secret game in the back room of The Claw? He doesn't drink much, and he's never been a gambler. He's so desperate to catch the killer, he will go to any lengths. I asked him about it, but he's being all secretive. I knew he was up to something, I just had no idea the danger he was putting himself in."

"Just as I'm sure he doesn't like the danger you keep putting yourself in, either," Trent pointed out. She knew he was only trying to help, but there was something in his tone that seemed different.

She pulled her hand from his and took another sip. "Yes, but I'm less than half my father's age, and I have you. He doesn't have anyone because he won't tell anyone what he's up to. That's a dangerous game for any man his age to be playing. For a man with his health issues, it's just plain stupid." She shook her head, feeling anger rise to the surface every time she thought about what this case was doing to her family. "Sheriff Evans was all too happy to bust up the party. After my father's heart attack, the sheriff let him off with just a warning as if he were doing us all a favor."

"He's just trying to get you both to back off and let him do his job," Trent said carefully, adding, "which isn't a bad idea I'm beginning to think."

Stacy's jaw fell open in surprise, her gaze locking onto his. So much for him being her rock. Now he was taking the side of the sheriff? That ticked her off bigtime. "You know I don't trust cops. I can't believe you would take his side over mine."

Trent frowned. "I'm not trying to take his side, I'm just saying things are getting a little out of control now. At least the police are trained to handle all sorts of situations while neither of you are." Trent didn't back down, his gaze unwavering. He reached out for her hand again, but she pulled away. He sighed and pushed his untouched glass away. "I don't know what I would do if something happened to you. I'm worried about you both."

"Well, no need." She sat up straight and squared her shoulders. "I'm beginning to think I can take care of myself."

He looked at her with exasperation. "I didn't say I wouldn't help you anymore."

"No need. You're just a delivery man, right?" She gave him a level look, but he didn't say a word like she suspected he wouldn't. Her father wasn't the only one who was keeping secrets and playing a dangerous game. "Last I checked delivery men weren't trained to handle these situations either," she added, then downed her drink defiantly, knowing she was being unreasonable but needing someone to act as her punching back before she suffocated on her frustration.

Trent stared at her, his gaze so hard to read sometimes. At times she felt as though she knew him better than anyone, yet in many ways he was still a mystery to her. She didn't really know that much about him, it just felt like she did. And there was one thing she knew for certain, that she'd needed him. Maybe she needed him too much, and that was the problem.

"Do you want me to stay with you?" he finally asked.

"No, I need to think." She didn't meet his eyes.

"Stacy—"

"I'm fine." She cut him off, afraid of what he might say. She had no intention of giving up looking for her mother's killer until justice was served.

Trent waited a beat, but she didn't say anything more. "Okay, then." He stood and headed for the door. "You know where I am if you need anything at all."

She nodded once and poured herself another. A moment later, he was gone. Damn him. This was what she had been afraid of. Needing someone too much, coming to rely on them and then being let down. She couldn't let him get too close. Not when she had so much to lose. Wiping away a tear, she dumped her drink down the drain and headed up to bed, hoping sleep would make her forget him if only for a little while.

An hour later she lay in bed wearing only a tank top and boxers. Her bedroom was upstairs so she deemed it safe to open the window. The cool evening breeze filled the room, carrying the scents of the sea with it. She listened to the rain softly falling on her roof as sleep evaded her. No matter how hard she tried, she couldn't get Trent off her mind or the disappointed look he'd given her as he'd walked out her door.

Maybe warm milk would help. Heading down into her kitchen, she poured milk into a small pot and stirred it as it slowly heated. She was used to living alone, yet staying with her father and then spending so much time with Trent had changed her, awakened her, made her realize what she was missing. Damn him for that.

She'd never realized how lonely she had been.

When the milk was warm, she poured it into a mug and turned the stove off. A clatter sounded out in the yard. She went to the window and peered out, then shook her head. The neighbor's dog had knocked her trash can over again, but it would have to wait until morning. She wasn't in the mood to get soaked. Finishing her milk, she set the mug in the sink and turned to head upstairs.

A gloved fist connected with her face, snapping her head back. A sharp pain exploded in her head, and she fell to the ground, clutching her eye and cheekbone. She fought to remain conscious, her head swimming as she tried to make sense of what had just happened.

Suddenly someone was on top of her with those same gloved hands wrapped tightly around her neck.

She opened her eyes, but her kitchen was black and the dark image before her had a stocking over its head. It was impossible to tell who it was and hard to think as her oxygen supply was being cut off. Lucky for her she could hold her breath for a long time. She clawed at the gloved fingers squeezing her throat.

Tears sprang to Stacy's eyes. She didn't want to die. Her father needed her, and she needed him. And if she were being honest, she needed Trent too. So much more than she realized. Searching her brain, she remembered her father teaching her self-defense after her mother had died. He didn't want her to go off to college without knowing how to defend herself. She wasn't getting anywhere trying to pry the hands from her throat. She needed leverage.

Clasping her hands together, she slipped them beneath the killer's arms and drove them up as she bucked her hips high and to the side. The person jerked in surprise and then tumbled to the left, his hands breaking free of Stacy's throat. She gasped for air, realizing she was free. Not hesitating, she scrambled to her feet and ran out her unlocked back door, grabbing the keys to her rental car along the way without looking back.

She could have sworn she'd locked her doors. She had started doing that the minute her mother's case was reopened and scary things had started happening. Rain ran down her face, but she felt numb, as if she were in shock. She functioned on auto pilot as she bolted into her car. Not even thinking about what to do or where to go, she put the car in drive and took off in just her tank top and boxers, bare feet and all, with no phone or purse. Moments later, she reached her destination.

Trent Clark's cottage.

Climbing out of her rental car, she ran to his door and pounded hard, knowing he always locked it. Suddenly she started to shake, her heart beating faster and breath coming in choppy gasps. Reality was setting in as cold hard truth of what had just happened to her hit her hard. It wasn't cold even though a soft rain was dampening her pajamas, yet she was chilled like the ocean after the spring thaw. Her teeth chattered, the shock over what had just happened to her taking its toll. A light finally came on inside the cottage, and she heard the lock turn. When the door finally opened, Trent's eyes widened, and that was all it took.

Stacy burst into tears.

137

STACY FELT LIKE AN IDIOT, standing half-naked in Trent's doorway, sobbing hysterically. It was too much: her father's heart attack, their argument earlier, and then getting attacked in her own home. She might be a strong woman, but this was ridiculous. Even *she* had her breaking point.

Trent had on a pair of athletic shorts and nothing else, as if he'd just rolled out of bed. He was an impressive man when fully dressed. Without a shirt, he was godlike: bronzed skin, sculpted muscles, a thin sprinkling of dark hair covering a broad chest. He ran a hand over his buzzed head and then his whiskered face, looking helpless for a moment as if trying to figure out what to do. Finally, he held open his big, capable arms, and Stacy didn't hesitate. She flew into them, hugging him close with her wet cheek pressed tightly against his chest. Trent pushed the door closed behind her and locked it, making her cry harder.

"Hey, easy now. It can't be that bad, can it?" he asked softly with his chin resting on top of her head.

"Y-Yes it can," she barely got out between sobs, clinging to the warmth of his body, inhaling his musky scent from the safe haven of his embrace.

He hesitated for only a moment before scooping her into his arms and carrying her to the couch in his living room. The cottage was small but cozy, with a stunning view of the ocean. He sat down on the plush material covering the thick cushion, bringing her with him to rest on his lap as he pulled an incredibly soft fleece throw over them. Holding her close, he rubbed her back for a long time with his wide palm, until her breathing settled and her tears subsided. She finally stopped shaking, the warmth of his bare skin against her thin tank top chasing the chill away, and his steady heartbeat reassuring her she was safe with every thump.

"You ready to tell me what happened yet?" His deep voice coaxed from somewhere near her ear.

Sitting up on his lap, she tightened the blanket around her shoulders as she looked him in the eyes. "I couldn't sleep after you left, so I got up and made some warm milk. I heard a noise outside, but I thought it was the neighbor's dog getting into our trash again. When I turned around, he was there. Before I knew what was happening, he was on me." Her eyes welled up again and she blinked against the pain in her eye. "Someone broke into my house tonight and attacked me."

Trent stiffened, his eyes going wide and lips parting. "Oh my God, are you okay?" His hands swept over her, and then paused on her cheekbone which had started to swell. "I didn't notice when you flew into me, and then your head was down as I held you. Your eye is already turning black." He clenched his teeth. After a moment of struggling for control, he finally said, "We need to call the police. I'll kill the son-of-a-bitch."

She grabbed his arms to still him when he would have stood up. "No."

His jaw bulged, and his muscles tensed as if ready to

spring into action. It took a minute for him to reign in his anger enough to say, "Stacy, this is serious."

She shook her head no. "What good would it do? I don't trust them. I have you. That's all I need. Besides, the guy's probably long gone by now." Her shoulders drooped. "It was my fault. I left the door unlocked. I feel like such a fool."

Trent closed his eyes for a moment. When he opened them, his gaze softened and he tucked an unruly curl behind her ear. "It was *not* your fault. Do you hear me? No one has the right to enter your home without your permission, and they sure as hell don't have the right to attack you." A muscle in his jaw pulsed again, and his gaze roamed over every inch of her. "What exactly did he do to you?"

"I know what you're thinking, but I'm okay. He didn't do anything like that. He just punched me in the face and then tried to strangle me. That's all."

"That's all? I'd say that's enough. Jesus, Stacy, I'm so sorry." Trent's features grew pinched as if physically in pain. "I should have been there. I should have protected you."

"How could you? I pushed you away, remember?" She looked at him, letting her regret shine in her eyes. "I'm the one who's sorry. I said I didn't need you. I was wrong." She took a shaky breath. "I was hurting so I lashed out at you, when you're the one thing I want more than anything else. It scares the hell out of me how much I want you."

He searched her eyes intensely. "Why?"

"Because I don't want to lose you, too, and please don't say that won't happen. We both know neither one of us plans to stick around for long."

He reached out and cupped her cheek, gently stroking the bruise. "You're right, we don't know what's going to happen in the future. No one does. But we're here together now." His gaze caressed her body and settled on her own gaze, holding her captive. "I want you, too, sweetheart. More than I ever thought possible." He swiped his thumb over her bottom lip. "I need you, Stacy."

She covered his hand with her own and kissed his palm.

"I know I don't talk about my personal life much, but it's not because I don't want to," he went on. "You're not the only one with issues. There's a lot going on in my life right now with my own family. I try to be strong and act like everything's fine, but it's not. I've been alone for a long time now. It's not always easy to let someone in."

Stacy could see the pain in his eyes. He was always there for her whenever she needed him. She never considered he might need her too. She suddenly wanted to be there for him. "You're not alone, Trent. You have me, and I'm not going anywhere."

Pushing back the blanket, she let it fall to her lap, revealing her thin tank top that had grown see-through from the rain. His gaze dropped to her chest in surprise, and then heated after her nipples hardened in response.

"Are you sure?" he asked in a voice filled with need, his muscles tense with restraint even though she could tell he wanted nothing more than to touch her. It made her dizzy with desire.

"I've never been more sure of anything." She picked up his hand and covered her breast with it as she leaned in to kiss him.

Trent groaned, deepening the kiss and thrusting his tongue into her mouth as he squeezed her gently and then fanned his thumb across her nipple. Stacy moaned as she straddled him, feeling the length of him harden beneath her. Grabbing the hem of her tank top, he slid the thin garment up, breaking their kiss long enough to slip it over her head.

"You're so damned beautiful," he whispered in awe before taking her nipple in his mouth.

Stacy arched her back, rotating her hips against him and running her hands over his head and shoulders. "Trent, oh God, I need you so much." She needed to feel alive again.

"I know, baby, me too." He rolled her to her back on the couch and pressed his muscular chest against hers as he settled his hips between her legs.

He kissed her lips, her face, her neck, and her breasts before working his way down her stomach. Butterflies fluttered beneath her skin. Stacy lifted her hips slightly, allowing him to pull her boxers off. He took a moment to worship her with his eyes as he gently stroked her, parting her folds and making her moan as his thumb found her most intimate spot. He made her feel beautiful and special. She gasped when she felt his tongue stroke over her before plunging deep and making her buck her hips in an age-old plea to be one with him.

No words were necessary.

He rolled off her to push his shorts down, allowing her a glimpse of the powerful length of him before sliding his arms beneath her knees to lift her legs high. His gaze locked onto hers, holding her captive as he slowly pressed into her until he was imbedded fully, joining them as one. No one had ever fit her like he did, as if he alone were meant for her and she him.

He stilled, his features strained in agony as he held back until her body welcomed him. She ran her fingernails down his chest on a shiver, letting him know it was okay, and that was all it took. He snapped. With a growl, he dropped to her chest and kissed her deeply as he began to move. Matching him stroke for stroke, she clung to him not wanting to ever let go. Being in his arms felt so right.

Maybe she really could have it all.

* * *

A POWERFUL FEELING filled Trent as he made love to Stacy, her scent of sunshine and honey filling his nostrils. It had been a long time since he'd been with a woman, but in all his years as a man, he'd never felt like this before. He wanted to protect her and cherish her and please her with little thought to his own needs. She was so responsive to his every touch, it turned him on like nothing else, bringing out a fierce need for her.

She'd scared the hell out of him, showing up on his doorstep so upset. Anger like he'd never known had seized him over the thought of someone harming a single hair on her precious head. When he found out who it was—and he *would* find the man—Trent would make him pay. What had started out as a personal mission had turned into so much more. He wanted to open up to her, tell her everything, but he was terrified it would ruin what they had built.

She trusted him.

That thought kept him up at night, but right now she needed him. He wouldn't let her down. Riding the wave of ecstasy with him, she suddenly grabbed his shoulders and arched her back as she screamed out his name. That was his undoing. He joined her, his body convulsing in pure pleasure until he stiffened on a moan and then collapsed on top of her, breathing heavily. He rolled to his back and brought her with him so his weight wouldn't crush her.

They lay there for a long moment, their naked limbs entwined with her breasts pressed against his chest as they cuddled. She felt so right in his arms, he didn't want this night to end. He didn't want reality to intrude because once it did, he would have to face the fact that the truth would come out and she would be gone.

"What's wrong?" she asked, sensing his shift in mood.

"I was just thinking how I didn't want this night to end."

"Who says it has to?" she asked with that warm buttered tone he'd come to love. And then she kissed him so hotly, all his fears about the future melted away.

* * *

THE NEXT DAY Mack got dressed in his standard jeans and t-shirt. He'd never been a shorts kind of man. Didn't really need to worry about that in northern Maine. He wondered if he would miss this place when he was gone. Probably, as it was all he'd ever known, but he had to leave. He couldn't bear the thought of those who knew and loved him watching him slowly fade away, and he wasn't just talking about Stacy.

Mack had known for a while now that Dr. Olivia Hurn had fallen in love with him. She'd never allowed herself to even consider looking at him in a romantic way when Elizabeth had been alive. They had been best friends. But after his Beth had died tragically, Liv had stepped in to help Mack when he'd needed it most, especially after Stacy had gone away to school and never came home.

In his own way Mack had grown to love Olivia, but not fully. His Elizabeth had never completely let go of his heart. He'd sometimes entertained a future with Olivia and wondered if what he could give her would be enough, but after he'd gotten sick, he hadn't wanted to burden her with watching him lose everything that was dear to him. Now that he'd found out Elizabeth had been murdered, he blamed himself. He didn't deserve to love or be loved by anyone because he'd let his queen down by not bringing her killer to justice. The bastard was targeting his daughter now. Whatever the cost, Mack couldn't let Stacy down, too.

"What do you think you're doing?" Dr. Hurn walked into his room, carrying his chart and giving him a disapproving look over the top of her fancy glasses.

"I'm going home." He finished tucking his shirt in and sat down on the bed to pull on his boots.

She lowered her glasses and let them hang from their chain as they rested on her immaculate lab coat. "No, you're not." He had to grin a little at her stubborn doctor expression, but she didn't fool him. She was a big softie beneath her straight-laced, no-nonsense, chicly packaged exterior.

"You don't scare me, Liv." He winked, making her flush like he knew it would. He planned to distract her in whatever way he could until he made his escape. He had plans, and he wasn't about to let her or his health interfere with them.

"I don't need to. You had a heart attack." She tapped her clipboard, stirring up her expensive smelling perfume. She always said she wore it because her patients deserved to smell something pretty instead of depressing antiseptic. Another thing he admired about her, but she wasn't sugar coating anything now as she added, "I'd say that's scary enough."

"Dying doesn't scare me, Doc." He stood to his full height of six-foot-seven, towering over her as he patted his chest. "Living without my memories is far more terrifying than this old ticker giving out."

"Oh, really." She raised a golden blonde brow, not backing down one inch. "Then how come you pressed the button for help?"

"Because I'm not finished living yet." He set his jaw

and nodded once. "There are a few more things this little old man has to do."

"You're not old, Mack." She looked him over, muttering beneath her breath, "And you're certainly not little."

"Tell you what. You can check up on me every day if it will make you feel better. I just need to go home."

"Oh, you can be sure of that, my friend." She pointed her finger at him. "For the record, you don't scare me either. Count on me calling you until you're so annoyed at the sound of my voice you'll give up this foolish quest and let me take care of you."

"I could never be annoyed at the sound of your voice," he said softly, meaning every single word. "And I promise I *will* call if I need you. I'll be careful, Liv. You have my word on that."

She stared at him for a long moment before finally responding, "Okay."

"Yeah?" He blinked, surprised she had given in without too much of a fuss.

"Yeah." She hugged him hard, surprising him even more. While he might have suspected her feelings for some time now, she had never given in to them. She really had been loyal and true to his wife, and he thanked the good Lord every day that his Beth had been so lucky. They both had. Olivia stepped back and finished with, "Your word's always been good enough for me, Mackenzie Buchanan."

Trent and Stacy walked into his room moments later, Olivia's jaw fell open as she stared with suspicion and shock, and Mack had the good grace to flush.

"You knew I'd say yes, didn't you?" Olivia narrowed her eyes at him.

Mack shrugged sheepishly, smart enough not to say anything, but they both knew it didn't matter. He had been going home either way.

"Are you sure he's okay?" Stacy asked the doctor, holding her hand up to silence him when he would object.

Dr. Hurn sighed. "Apparently so. Just do me a favor and keep a close eye on this one. He's slippery."

"Don't you worry," Stacy said, giving him a hard look as if she'd taken lessons from Liv. "I'm not letting him out of my sight."

"Speaking of patients, can you take a look at her, Doc?" Trent spoke up, earning a sharp look from Stacy.

"I told you I'm fine," Stacy whispered to Trent, but Mack heard.

"Wait, did something else happen?" Mack stepped forward, studying his daughter more closely. She was suspiciously avoiding his gaze. He leaned down until Stacy had no choice but to look him in the eye.

"Thanks, Trent," she grumbled.

"I can't help but worry about you," Trent said in a soft voice that matched the look in his eyes and revealed so much.

Dr. Hurn harrumphed. "Welcome to my world."

"What aren't you telling me, Stacy Marie?" Mack crossed his arms in a stance that brooked no argument. Now that he thought about it, she had on more makeup than he remembered her wearing, and she was dressed a little fancier than she normally did. He'd just assumed they were going someplace together. It was clear they fancied each other. Now he had to wonder if there was more to it.

Stacy rolled her eyes. "It's no big deal, really, but someone broke into the house last night."

"What?" Mack barked, clenching his fists. He would kill the bastard.

"Dad, your heart." Stacy looked concerned, rushing to his side. "This is why I wasn't going to say anything." She glared at Trent.

"Stacy, if something happened to you, then you need to tell the police." Dr. Hurn studied her closely.

"That's what I tried to tell her." Trent held his hands up. "Stubbornness seems to run in their family."

"Fine." Stacy pulled off the silky scarf she had draped for show over her blouse, revealing dark bruises on her neck in the shape of fingers. "Someone punched me in the face and tried to strangle me, but like I said, I'm fine."

"Like hell you are," Mack growled, a fury he'd never known filling him to his core. This was his baby girl. She was the only part of Elizabeth he had left. He'd be damned if he would let anything happen to her, too.

"Mack..." Dr. Hurn stared him down, holding up her clipboard. "Don't make me rip up these release forms."

"I'm fine, but this situation is getting out of hand." Mack sat down, breathing deeply and slowing his heart rate. She was right. He needed to stay healthy long enough to finish what he had started. "Obviously Elizabeth's killer is still on the loose and dangerous. Something has to be done."

"Agreed," Trent chimed in.

"Shhhhh, everyone quiet." Stacy swiped her hand through the air, staring at the TV in shock. "I think something just was."

"What are you talking about?" Mack asked, confused.

His daughter pointed to the television set and read the headline. "Breaking news. Sheriff Evans just arrested someone for the murder of Elizabeth Buchanan." Tears filled Stacy's eyes as she looked at him with hope and relief. "I think this nightmare is finally over with, Dad. Mom's killer has just been caught."

14

SHERIFF EVANS STOOD outside of the county courthouse, preparing to hold a press conference. He was going to see to it that Stacy Buchanan was done stirring up trouble in his town. Most of the citizens had shown up, forcing the conference to be held outside. It was a good thing the weather had cooperated, unlike the day before when it had poured. It was about the only thing cooperating with him these days. The last thing he needed was for the word *murder* to scare folks away. Coldwater Cove counted on the money tourists brought in to fund all its programs.

Thinking a killer was still on the loose was bad for business.

Not to mention Stacy was putting herself in danger, scaring everyone into thinking Coldwater Cover wasn't a safe place to raise a family anymore. He was receiving pressure from the public to do something. He wasn't stupid. All these so-called accidents hadn't started until she moved back home and poked her nose into places it didn't belong.

This was *his* town. He knew everything.

She might not have told him about the break-in at her house, but he had his spies. He'd heard about it before the rain was dry on her roof. Why hadn't she reported it? Instead she'd run to the delivery man she'd been spending time with. Rory didn't trust Trent Clark. He'd been in law enforcement long enough to know when someone was hiding something.

Rory had decided to take matters into his own hands. He'd told the mayor he wasn't about to take the fall alone. If his secrets came out, so would others. Mayor Zuckerman wasn't above turning on anyone if it meant keeping his own ass safe. Together they had found the perfect scapegoat to pin Elizabeth Buchanan's murder on.

Case closed.

Rory tapped the microphone as he stood on the courthouse steps. "Excuse me, is this thing on?" The microphone screeched loudly, and he flinched, shooting a sharp glance at the AV guy.

Sorry, sir, the man mouthed and quickly made some adjustments, then gave him a thumb's up.

"Thank you for gathering here today." Rory spoke close to the mic, and the rumble of conversation quieted. "I'm sure most of you are aware that there was an arrest in Elizabeth Buchanan's murder case." Hushed voices hummed through the crowd. "I wanted to reassure you personally that Coldwater Cove is a safe place to be. Soo Young Lee is behind bars and won't be hurting anyone else in this lifetime."

The second he finished speaking, reporters started hammering him with questions like he knew they would. It didn't bother him. This was his job as sheriff, and it made him feel important. Besides, Soo was guilty of a crime. Maybe not murder, but she still deserved to go to jail. His conscience could live with that. At least with the case closed, his secrets were safe and Stacy would leave town.

"Sheriff Evans, how do you know for sure that Soo

'Young Lee is the killer?" A young woman obviously eager to make a name for herself thrust a camera in his direction.

He stood straighter and angled his head in a way that he knew made him look good. "I can't discuss the details of the case because the investigation is still ongoing, but I can tell you we have the evidence we need to gain a conviction."

"Can you tell us what the evidence is, Sheriff?" another reporter asked.

"I'm not at liberty to say. The point of this press conference is to let you all know you are safe. There's no more need for anyone to get involved. Let us do our job and close this case. Enjoy the rest of your summer, folks."

Sheriff Evans took a few more questions and then the mayor stepped up to the mic. When the sheriff stepped down, he had hoped to make a clean getaway, but he should have known better. He was pulled aside by Stacy Buchanan, her father, and Trent Clark. The man was everywhere, sticking his nose in where it didn't belong.

"Sheriff, can I have a moment of your time?" Stacy asked as she stepped in front of him, flanked on both sides by the men in a unified front.

Having no choice, Rory stopped. "Look, Ms. Buchanan. You asked me to do my job, and that's what I'm trying to do. If you'll excuse me, I have a case to close. I would think you would be happy about that." He tried to step around her.

"Wait, just hear me out, please." She stepped in front of him once more. "It's about my mother's case and it's important, or I promise I wouldn't be bothering you. I want to be sure you arrested the right person."

That got his attention. "I'm listening."

She pulled off her scarf—almost reluctantly—to reveal dark bruises around her throat. "I was attacked last night in my own home by a man. Soo Young Lee is a woman."

He feigned surprise. "I'm sorry to hear that. Why didn't you report it immediately?"

She had the good grace to flush. "Because I was afraid."

He thought about what she said before asking, "How do you know your attacker was a man? Did you see his face?"

"Well, no, I guess I just assumed." Stacy frowned, and he could see the wheels in her head spinning. "Now that I think about it, I'm not sure why I did that. The person was average sized so I guess it could have been a man or a woman." Good. He'd instilled doubt, and hopefully that would be enough.

"A lot of people are average height, including Ms. Lee. You've made a number of enemies in this town, Ms. Buchanan," Rory said in his most professional, objective tone. "Your attacker could have been someone with a grudge against you, man or woman. You said you never saw the person who chased you in the woods or ran you off the road or cut the tree, either. Trust me when I say Ms. Lee is your mother's killer. She had motive and no alibi. Now that she is apprehended, I'm sure you will be safe."

"Trust doesn't come easy in regards to your department," Mack Buchanan grumbled. "We need more than just your word from you. You owe our family that much if you expect us to let this case go. Since this case involves my deceased wife and now my daughter, I think you can make an exception."

If Rory didn't give them something, they would never stop hounding him or snooping around on their own. He looked around and then led them over to a secluded tree before speaking. "Years ago during your wife's term, her office had come under suspicion when the books didn't match the amount of money spent on the youth program. The mayor was questioned as you know, but she died tragically before any evidence was found. After her death the youth program was suspended and a scholarship created in her name. Now that it was discovered your wife was murdered and her case reopened, new evidence has come to light."

"Can you tell us more about the evidence, Sheriff?" Trent Clark asked.

"Who exactly are you, by the way?" Rory asked. The man seemed to be everywhere lately.

"A friend of the family who is only trying to help," Stacy interjected. "You were saying, Sheriff?"

"Look, this is what we know. Your mother put Ms. Lee in charge of the youth programs. When your mother discovered funds were missing, she confronted Ms. Lee and had planned to fire her. Ms. Lee wrote the blackmail note you showed me, threatening to lie about the mayor's involvement and ruin the program unless your mother met her in private at Mariner's Marina. Your mother showed up, and Ms. Lee killed her to keep her quiet with no one the wiser. Case closed."

"How do you know this?" Mack narrowed his eyes in suspicion.

"Mayor Zuckerman kept Ms. Lee on, thinking she was a rising star. It wasn't until the case was reopened and I asked him to look into his office's old records more closely that he found the proof. Ms. Lee has confessed to stealing and laundering money from the mayor's office for years, but denies killing your wife. However, I am confident the truth will come out during her trial. You didn't hear any of this from me. Now if you don't mind, I really must go." Rory walked away before they could ask any more questions, hoping he'd said enough. Because if they didn't buy the story he was selling, he'd be forced to resort to Plan B.

And Plan B wouldn't be good for anyone.

* * *

RELIEF SURGED THROUGH ME, nearly bringing me to my knees as I stood in the crowd of people right up front. This was my town. I would never hide. I deserved to be front and center. Lord knew I had certainly earned it, paying the ultimate price for that right. I wouldn't give it up easily, and maybe now I wouldn't have to. The sheriff had arrested Elizabeth Buchanan's killer. Finally the nightmare was over. It didn't matter that I knew the truth. I knew who the *real* killer was.

Me.

That secret would go with me to my grave. I swallowed hard, tasting acid. My stomach had been in knots with the thought of actually taking a life with my own two hands. Since the accidents weren't working, I had tried to remove the threat myself. My hands shook with the memory of trying to squeeze the life out of Stacy Buchanan. I'd caught her by surprise as planned and had nearly broken her neck.

I shuddered as I remembered feeling her bones strain beneath my fingers. Bile had hit the back of my throat over the thought of what it would feel like it they snapped in half and my fingers pushed through her skin. I probably would have gotten sick, but that wouldn't do. Vomit would reveal my DNA. It had almost been a relief when she'd managed to escape my grasp. She was a strong one, athletic, but I was stronger. Still, I liked helping people now, not hurting them. Helping people felt good. Hurting people came with regrets, but sometimes it was a necessary evil.

Except now I didn't have to anymore.

I took a deep breath, smiling and waving to the citizens of Coldwater Cove. They all knew me, looked up to me, respected me. They had no clue what I had done in my past, and they never would. Not as long as I lived and breathed and could do something about it.

I was living proof that one could never truly know thy neighbor.

* * *

"ARE you sure everything is all set?" Mack asked his lawyer, Louis Vito, as he sat across from him in his plush office.

Prestigious awards hung on the walls, thick shag carpet covered the floor, and overstuffed chairs were strategically placed for comfort. His sidebar housed fine china for coffee mugs and tea cups, with fancy crystal water, wine, and whiskey glasses. The man was into fine wine, expensive liquor, and pricey cigars. He owned his own practice and pretty much did what he wanted whenever he wanted. Imbibing in the afternoon wasn't out of the question, but he was damn good at his job.

Mack had never questioned his integrity when it came to the law.

"I made all the changes you asked me to. The youth program will be able to start back up and the charity in Elizabeth's name will be funded for years to come. As for Stacy and Dr. Hurn, they will both be taken care of. You know that neither one of them would want you to give your money to them since they both work and can support themselves, right?"

Mack shrugged. "Doesn't matter. By the time they find out, it will be too late and they will just have to accept it."

Louis slid a copy of Mack's latest will over to him,

looking as though he was deciding whether or not to speak his mind. "You sure about all of this? How are you going to retire if you give everything away?"

"Yes I'm sure. I've made up my mind. I don't want to hold Stacy back. She has dreams and plans that don't involve Coldwater Cove, but I would never be happy at Whispering Pines. Dr. Hurn will never move on unless I'm gone. And where I'm going, I won't need any money. I've already paid my dues. Trust me it's a better place."

Louis looked a little confused and curious, but he didn't press the matter. "I get it." He stared at a picture hanging on his wall, and the expression on his face transformed into one of serenity mixed with a bit of sadness. "See that lake?"

Mack glanced at the scenic photo of a gorgeous two story log cabin with a wall of windows facing a placid lake nestled inland in the woods, its reflection staring back at him enticingly. He nodded. "It's really nice."

"Oh, it's more than nice. That's *my* better place," Louis said wistfully. "Or at least it will be when my divorce is settled. Gary Sanders sold us that house. That man has a gift for making things happen. If you want to sell, he'll find you a buyer. If you want a place out in the middle of nowhere, he'll find the perfect spot. I'm sure he'll sell your house before you know it, and you'll get to go to your better place."

"I'm sure you're right."

"I sure do love my place, but my wife doesn't love me. She knows I would hand over anything she wanted except for that, just to be finished with her, but she's fought me tooth and nail for a year now. She hates that place. Says it reminds her of me. She doesn't even live there, she just doesn't want me to have it. No one lives there now, which is a damn shame, but all that's about to change." A gleam of determination entered his eyes.

"I've worked too long and hard not to get what I deserve."

"I hope you do, Louis. It's important to be happy." Mack studied his friend. He'd been his lawyer for years, but he didn't really associate with him outside of his office. Mack had no idea Louis was getting a divorce, and Mack suddenly realized he didn't know as much as he thought he did about the man. "I'm sorry about your wife," he added.

"Don't be. She only loved me for my money. Can't say as I blame her. I can admit that I loved my vices a lot more than my wife." Louis shrugged. "Oh well, c'est la vie. My dog on the other hand adores me. There truly is no greater loyalty and love than man's best friend. He's all I need, and well, maybe a date with a fishing pole occasionally." Louis winked.

"Amen." Mack stood. "Thank you, my friend. It's been a pleasure doing business with you. Be seeing you."

"Anytime." Louis stood to join him. "You doing okay? You seem different. A little down."

"Just getting old."

"Aren't we all?" They both laughed. "You be careful now. Take care of yourself, and be sure to find a new doctor wherever you're going."

"Will do," Mack said as he walked out the door, knowing full well he would do no such thing. He was done with doctors and hospitals and Alzheimer's and heart attacks.

He was done with it all.

15

"I REALLY THOUGHT the killer was a man," Stacy said while rubbing her sore neck a few days later. Her eye was purple and yellow now. No amount of makeup was hiding that. Nothing more had happened to her, so they must have caught the real killer. She sat across from her father at the kitchen table, sipping herbal tea with honey. "I had been so positive. Usually my instincts are right."

Then again she had thought Trent Clark was hiding something, but he had been her rock. She had thought she didn't need anyone, but she seriously didn't know if she could have gone through everything that had happened to her without him by her side. It was uncanny how he always appeared exactly when she needed him most.

Her father was reading the newspaper while drinking his coffee black. "Soo Young Lee," he mulled the words over as if testing how they rolled off his tongue, and then shook his head. "I don't know. Something just doesn't seem right."

Stacy reached out and covered his hand with her own. She would miss moments like this, had already missed too many. "I know it's hard to let go, Dad, but we have both held on too long to Mom's ghost. I think we did it because we both had known something was off in calling her death an accident. She wouldn't have gone anywhere near the water unless she'd had a good reason. And now we know why." Stacy didn't know who she was trying to convince more: herself or her father. All she knew for certain was she needed this all to be over.

"I suppose you're right," he muttered, as if trying to convince himself but not really succeeding.

"Gary Sanders called." She changed the subject and watched her father stiffen. He pushed the eggs around on his plate, and then slid the untouched breakfast away, returning to his newspaper.

"Yeah? What did he want," he said casually while flipping to the next page in the paper as if he didn't already know what was coming.

"Oh, just that you got an offer on the house." Stacy sipped her tea, watching him closely. She couldn't eat any more than he could. She hadn't wanted to bring it up, but she had known this day was coming. The day when the case would close and the house would sell and she would have to move on.

Her father grunted. "It's only the first offer. Maybe we should wait. See if anyone else is interested. Hold out for more."

"It's a good offer, Dad."

"Yeah, but I don't want just anyone living in our house." His eyes met and locked onto hers. "It's more than just a house. It's our home."

"A house is just a house," she said gently. "A home is family. Together we'll always be home no matter where we are. The people who made the offer are a young couple just starting out and expecting their first baby. Let it be a home to them now."

He sat there quiet for a long while, as if weighing

something heavy over. Finally his gaze met hers and he said, "Okay, Stac. Okay."

She blinked. "Okay? Really? Just like that?"

"It's hard letting go, but it's time."

"Does that mean you'll move into Whispering Pines?"

"Let's accept the offer on the house first." His eyes traveled around the kitchen, admiring the new touches and lingering wistfully on the pieces of their past. His eyes grew a little misty. "That will give me some time to say goodbye before we close."

"You'll be right in town, Dad. It's not like you'll never see the old place again." She laughed uneasily, trying to stay strong and not break down in front of him.

If only he would live with her, that would solve everything, she kept thinking. But even she knew he would need more care than she would be able to give very soon. He'd fought her every step of the way, but now he was oddly calm and acting strange. He'd been acting strange for a while.

"Old. I know all about being old. Too bad your young fella can't fix me up just as easily." Her father winked at her.

Stacy knew he was trying to lighten the mood and put her at ease. She would play along for his sake. "Trent's good, Dad, but I don't know if he's *that* good."

"Hey, now." Her father chuckled.

"Besides, he's not my fellow," she said, happy to change the subject.

Her father studied her closely, their years of separation fading away like the mist over the sea. He knew her better than she knew herself. "But you want him to be, don't you?"

"I don't know. I never thought marriage and children was something I wanted, but then I saw Laura again. She looks so happy."

"Ah Laura." Genuine warmth and pleasure transformed her father's face. He was still so strong and handsome, it was sometimes hard to believe he was sick. "Does Trent make you happy?" he asked, breaking into her thoughts.

She nodded. "I've never felt this way before. He's so kind and gentle and there for me. I know he's attracted to me, but beyond that, I just don't know. He's going through some issues of his own that he won't talk about. It's so frustrating. You and mom shared everything. I want to help him like he's helped me."

"Apparently we didn't share everything. She never told me where she was going that day," her father pointed out gently. "Your mother loved me. I don't doubt that for a minute, but sometimes people do things to protect the ones they love. Have you told Trent how you feel?"

"Not in so many words." This time Stacy was the one who couldn't meet her father's eyes. She didn't want him to see the fear of love that she had because of how the loss of his love had affected him. The last thing he needed was to blame himself for her not wanting to take a chance on love. She couldn't bear the thought of a life of sadness and loneliness if she lost that love like he did.

"Maybe it's time you told him," her father said as if reading her mind. "Being alone can be just as sad and lonely. Maybe I'm not the only one who needs a fresh start. Change is scary, believe me I know, but it wouldn't be worth having if it wasn't."

He was so right. She'd never really thought about it like that. Clearing the emotion from her throat, she leaned over and hugged him tight. "Thanks, Dad. I love you."

"Love you too, kiddo." He squeezed her hard and held on longer than normal. "Always remember that when I'm gone."

She leaned back and looked at him with confusion. He couldn't possibly be saying what she thought he was. "Where are you going?"

"My mind." He tapped his head. "I meant when my mind is gone. Must be it's going already." He smirked.

She gave him a look that said, *Not funny.* Then she took his hands in hers and tried to convey everything she felt. She needed him to know how sincere she was. "Don't worry, Dad. I won't let you forget. I'll tell you stories every day. I'm not going anywhere as long as you still need me." She realized she meant it. If he wasn't going with her, then she would stay here for him for as long as she needed to. To hell with her career. He was the most important thing in her life, and she planned to treasure whatever time they had left. "We don't have to sell the house."

"That's my girl. I knew you would say that, and I love you for it, but like I said...it's time. I'm sure I'll get plenty of help wherever I end up. You need to start living. Make a life of your own, Stac. Go be great like I always knew you could. I'll be right here."

His words were meant to reassure, but the niggling fear that something wasn't right settled deep into her chest. The problem was she didn't have a clue how to fix it.

* * *

TRENT PARKED his truck at Coldwater Cove marina in the middle of the night, scanning the docks, watching the area closely. Same as he had been for weeks. He'd been looking for suspicious activity between the Coast Guard and the harbormaster, who kept meeting more frequently than usual. It was tourist season, which meant fishing boats didn't just fish. Many chartered tours for extra money. Still, boats didn't usually sail out at odd hours like the middle of the night.

Trent had been staking out the marina during any free time in between helping Stacy solve her mother's murder. Now that her mother's case was closed, Trent had focused solely on his mission. He hadn't seen much of Stacy, and not because he didn't want to. It was getting harder to be around her and not tell her everything. If he could finish what he'd started, then maybe he could finally have a life of his own. He wanted a life, dammit. More than he'd ever thought possible. He'd spent the past decade living for someone else. It was his turn. He deserved some happiness. He might not have been looking for it, but he'd found it.

He was in love with Stacy Buchanan.

He knew she had her guard up when it came to love, but after the other night, he knew she had feelings for him, too. There was no way they could have shared that kind of connection and have it not be love. If he could finish his mission, he would come clean and then spend the rest of his life trying to make it up to her. Because once she found out who he was, she would never forgive him.

Trent was about to leave when he caught the dark shadow of a fishing boat cruising into the harbor at a slow speed with its lights off. His heart sped up. This could be the break he'd been looking for. Trent got out of his truck and closed the door quietly. Sticking to darting behind objects and staying in the darkness, he made his way silently down to the docks. A man tied the fishing vessel up and scurried off, too far away to see clearly. Trent gave chase, but the man disappeared beneath the cover of darkness, no moon or stars in sight, to make his escape through some buildings.

Dammit! Trent lost him.

Doubling back, he read the name of the boat. *The Queen*. Frowning, he wracked his brain for where he had heard that name before. His eyes widened as he realized that was the name of Mack's old boat. What the hell was it doing out on the ocean during the middle of the night? More importantly, who was the guy he'd seen skulking away like a criminal?

A movement at the base of the dock in the water caught Trent's eye. Maybe the guy had come back for something. Ducking behind a dumpster, ignoring the rotting fish smell, he peeked around the edge and frowned. He might not have seen the other man up close, but his gut told him this wasn't him. A man with red hair and a beard was checking the boat over. Trent had met Mack's old crew members, Roy and Wally. He'd heard about some new guy named Kurt, but he had yet to meet the man. This must be him. Mack had said he was older and had red hair and that he was surprised Roy had hired the man at his age. What was the guy doing down at the docks this time of night?

Nothing good, that was for sure.

Trent crept forward as the man climbed on board. He needed to see if anything was up there. This boat was the perfect sized vessel to smuggle cigarettes and firearms over to Canada and smuggle drugs back in. Given the boat had just come back in, the drugs were either still on board or most likely the drop off point was somewhere secluded by the shore. Maine waters were so deep along its rocky coast, the boat could get close and could easily transfer the drugs to the contact person on shore and then pull into the harbor, no one the wiser.

Trent climbed the ladder as carefully as he could, the boat rocking gently and slapping water against the dock. He stopped at the top to peek over the edge but didn't see anyone. Maybe the man was down in the cabin. Trent climbed over the back of the boat, landing with soft feet, having grown up around boats. That didn't do him much good as he only took one step before freezing. He was being watched. A noise sounded, and then everything happened at lightning speed. The boat surged wildly, and the man appeared before Trent in an instant.

"Freeze, FBI, put your hands up where I can see them," Trent shouted as he pulled his gun.

The red headed man had said and done the same thing. With guns trained on each other, recognition dawned simultaneously.

"Hello, Trent," the man said in a familiar voice.

That voice had never ceased to instill so many emotions in Trent: love, pride, sadness, disappointment, anger. He had thought there was something oddly familiar about the man, even at a distance. It didn't matter that his eyes were brown—probably from contacts—instead of green now. Trent would recognize them anywhere.

"Dad?" Trent asked almost in disbelief, knowing it was him but having a hard time wrapping his brain around how and why he was here.

They both lowered their weapons and just stared at each other, the boat creaking beneath their feet. There were so many things they both probably wanted to say, but neither quite knew how to start or what to do. The last time they had spoken, they'd had a huge fight.

"What's with the red hair and beard," Trent finally asked as he sheathed his gun, not really knowing how to start the conversation.

His father shrugged, doing the same. "It's my disguise."

"For what?" The night was eerily calm, the only sound the soft lap of water against the hull. "You're retired and not supposed to be here, Dad. Or did you forget?"

"Not by choice, and you know that. Talk about me? Trent Clark the Worldwide Parcel Delivery man? What are *you* up to?"

Trent bit back what he wanted to say and took a moment to count to ten. He was tired of arguing with his father. "I'm trying to prove what you couldn't ten years ago. That illegal dealings were happening on the docks in Coldwater Cove. The jury's still out on whether Mack or Elizabeth Buchanan knew anything about it. I hope for Stacy's sake that they didn't, but my loyalty has always been to you, Dad. I want vindication for you as much as for me. This case ruined both our lives."

His dad's shoulders drooped a little, and he hung his head. "I'm sorry about that, son. I truly am." He met his gaze head on and filled his words with conviction. "But all that's behind me. I haven't had a drink in weeks. It feels good to be clearheaded. I feel useful again. Do you know what that means to a man like me?"

His father had been a strong, proud man who took his job seriously and gave everything he had to it. As a result he defined his self-worth according to it. "I thought Stacy said you refused to help her?"

"I was afraid, but I changed my mind. She doesn't know. I wanted to right some wrongs first and see if I could catch her mother's killer at the same time. But I saw on the news she's already been caught. Nice work."

"That wasn't me. That was all Sheriff Evans."

"Stacy know who you are?" His father eyed him curiously. "I heard you two have been spending a lot of time together."

"No, she doesn't know." Trent averted his gaze. "I needed to get close to her family, but I planned to tell her as soon as this mission was finished. Speaking of that, did you find anything on board?"

His father gave him a knowing look but let it drop. "No."

"Any idea who the man was that took the boat out?"

His father was already shaking his head, and he looked troubled. "No, but the only ones with a key are myself and Roy and Wally."

"And Mack," Trent pointed out.

"You think he would sneak the boat out to do something illegal? What gain would he have?"

"Not sure." Trent puckered his brow. "All I know is he seems to be spending a lot of money lately, and he has been acting strange."

"I sure hope for his daughter's sake you're wrong." His father's gaze met and held his. "And for your own."

Trent inhaled a deep breath. "Only one way to find out. Care to end this thing together, Special Agent Robert West?"

Pride and feeling worthy took ten years off his father's face as he replied, "I thought you'd never ask."

Trent's chest tightened, and suddenly everything was worth it. He'd waited a long time to see his father like this. Like the man he'd worshipped his whole life. Stacy knew a little about what that was like. He sure as hell hoped his actions wouldn't ruin things with her, but there were some things that were out of his control. He'd learned a long time ago to let go.

Whatever was meant to happen would happen.

16

"YOU DONE GOOD, BOY," Charlie Wentworth said a couple days later as dawn covered the cove with a morning mist. "We've been trying to find out who the smuggler was for quite some time. I knew Granger worked for Buchanan, and that it wasn't a pretty ending, but I never imagined his hatred after being let go would run so deep. To make a copy of his key to *The Queen* and use her in smuggling runs goes against the lobster fisherman's code. They're fiercely loyal to their own, but Granger's always been a loose cannon."

"Thank you, sir." Trent shook his hand. "Just doing my job."

He and his father had staked out the marina in the middle of the night for days, waiting for the smuggler to make another run. That night had finally paid off. They'd made their move, relief filling Trent when he realized who the guilty culprit was. He'd just had no idea so many other organizations were looking for the smugglers.

"Special Agent Trent West. Who would have guessed?" Charlie shook his head in wonder, huffing and puffing as he waddled out of his office and led the way down to the waterfront.

All sorts of law enforcement agencies and media had descended upon the scene and taken over. Trent had already briefed them and gave a press release to the media, glad to be done with the case and ready to get on with his life.

"I have to say I would never have guessed you were working on the same case with the Coast Guard," Trent responded. "Honestly, I thought maybe you were also involved in something shady with all those deliveries. Especially because you weren't using your own law enforcement."

"Bah, the sheriff's department has been turning a blind eye for decades to the goings-on in the marina. That's why I started working with the Coast Guard. I've been around for a long time, son. Not much gets by me, but I'm no spring chicken." He patted his large belly. "I knew I needed help. I kept gathering logs and evidence of whatever I had and shared it with my connections through WPS. It was the only way I knew for sure it would stay secure. The sheriff's got eyes and ears everywhere."

"Smart." Trent nodded, admittedly impressed. He'd judged the harbormaster too quickly. He should have known better, probed sooner, and maybe they could have worked together.

"I had hoped when Pratt retired that Evans would be different, but he's been Pratt's lapdog for years. Too ambitious for his own good. It's a shame. The boy didn't start out that way. The mayor's office is no better. Elizabeth Buchanan wasn't like that. Her husband either, no matter what your old man might have thought." Charlie's eyes narrowed suspiciously. "Speaking of him, what's he been up to lately?"

"Don't know." Trent kept his features neutral, having prepared himself for these types of questions so he wouldn't be caught off guard. "I haven't seen or talked to him in years since he was ordered to stay out of Coldwater Cove. He wasn't the same man after that. He pushed us all away."

Trent and his father had both agreed to keep his disguise a secret. His father really didn't look anything like his old self. He would continue to be Roy's new stern man until he didn't need him anymore, since it was the right thing to do. Besides, he was enjoying himself, enjoying being clean, and enjoying his son. When he was ready, he would retire for real this time. His mission had been accomplished in proving he hadn't been crazy back then. Coldwater Cove was corrupt, and Elizabeth Buchanan had been murdered. A weight had been lifted from his shoulders now, and that was enough. He'd disappeared and let Trent call in the authorities, taking all the glory. He insisted he didn't want any credit, saying it didn't make up for being a crappy father, but it was a start.

"That was another damn shame." A look of pity crossed over Charlie's features. "Bob West was a fine man and a good cop, trying to do the right thing, but the cards were stacked against him. He didn't deserve everything that happened to him."

"No, he didn't. Thank you for recognizing that." Trent gave the man a nod.

"He's not the only good cop. Now, thanks to you, this town will have a fresh start. Evans and Zuckerman have been removed from office and Pratt has been summoned home. Those three will face judgment for their actions, and Elizabeth Buchanan's efforts to make the streets of the Cove safe will finally come to fruition. You're a good man, Trent. Don't let the job make you so hard that you forget that." He clapped Trent on the shoulder. "Maybe now I can finally retire and get on with my life knowing the town I love so much is in good hands."

Getting on with his life was exactly what Trent West planned to do. He had a new mission now, and that started with talking to Stacy Buchanan before someone else did. He started heading toward the parking lot but stopped in his tracks.

Well, hell.

Too late. The question now was would he have someone to share that new life with or would he be forever alone and lonely?

* * *

"How could you?" Stacy came to a stop in front of Trent, blocking his path. She wore an old pair of shorts and a t-shirt, her hair a wild tangled mess, and no makeup. She'd literally run out of the house after just getting up, not taking time to do anything other than slip on a pair of flip flops. "I can't believe you didn't tell me you were FBI. You knew how I felt about cops. And not just any cop. You're Robert West's son! You must have thought me a fool when I cried on your shoulder about your father not wanting to help me. I feel like such an idiot."

"Stacy, please understand. I wanted to tell you," Trent said, sounding full of regret. "In fact, that's where I was headed now."

He stood before her in boots, jeans and a polo shirt untucked and loose, undoubtedly to hide the holster, badge, and gun she knew must be attached to his pants. He needed a shave, his whiskers heavy and his buzzed hair needing a trim. He looked tired, the lines at the corners of his eyes deeper than normal, and faint shadows lingered beneath his eyes.

Everything about him looked so different now. How had she missed the signs? She should have listened to her gut, trusted her instincts that he was hiding something. He'd said he'd had family issues, too, but he hadn't trusted her enough to talk to her about them. That hurt the most. After everything they had been through, he should have at least given her the option of taking his side. He'd just assumed she wouldn't.

The fact that Bob West was his father wasn't the problem. Trent had *lied* to her. He'd broken her trust when he'd been the only person she could truly count on. All along he'd been digging through her mother's things and prying into her father's past to see what the FBI had been looking into years ago. If her father had been involved, Trent wouldn't have thought twice about taking him from her, too.

Had anything between them been real?

"You say you wanted to tell me, but you didn't," she said, her voice cracking with the pain she couldn't quite hide. "I had to hear about your real identity on the TV. Breaking news, Special Agent Trent West breaks up a decade old smuggling ring using my father's old boat. No wonder why you were so eager to help me. You didn't care about catching my mother's killer. All you cared about was finishing what your father had started."

"Not all cops are bad, Stacy," he replied, his voice filled with frustration. "I couldn't say anything until the case was closed. I was going to tell you, I swear, but I couldn't risk my cover being blown." His hands were on his hips, his spine ramrod straight as he leaned in toward her. "Yes, dammit! I wanted vindication for my old man, okay? It's all I've thought about for ten goddamned years. You of all people should get that." His hazel eyes blazed anger, frustration, and hopelessness as they bore into hers.

"Oh, don't you dare go there. I get that, and no I don't blame you for standing up for your father. I would expect nothing less from you. What I *don't* understand is how you could use me to get your vindication. Tell me so I can try and understand this." She looked at him with disgust. "What the hell did fucking me get you?"

He clenched his jaw and a muscle bulged as he fought for restraint. "Not a goddamned thing, apparently. We didn't *fuck*; we made love. You're just too scared to admit it. Jesus, Stacy, I tried to keep my distance. So did you, as I recall. There's a reason neither of us could. Can't you see that?" He took several deep breaths and then the anger left him like air leaving a sail. His features softened and his eyes filled with sadness as he said tenderly, "I love you, Stacy Buchanan, whether you want to hear that or not. Neither one of us was free to live until these cases were closed." He reached a hand toward her, his eyes filled with hope.

Stacy stepped out of his reach before she caved into the tone of his voice and the look in his eyes. God, all she wanted to do was lean in and let him wrap her in his arms. She needed him. Dammit, why'd he have to go and make her fall in love with him? Tears welled up in her eyes, but she blinked them back, choking on emotion.

"Well, that sucks for you because I don't love you. I hate you and never want to see you again. How's that for closing a case?"

* * *

"Nothing is what it seems anymore. The whole town is falling apart," Mack said to Soo Young Lee as he sat across from her in the jail's visiting room. She was awaiting trial before learning her fate. She was going to prison. The question was for how long? It all depended on her cooperation.

"I heard," she said quietly. "Can't say that I'm surprised."

Her black hair was pulled back in a simple ponytail, her face makeup free, making her look like the kid she'd been when she'd first come to Elizabeth for a job. It was a shame her life had taken such a drastic turn. She'd had so much potential.

"If it's any consolation, I'm sorry," she added, her voice cracking with emotion, giving Mack hope that his instincts were right.

"For what? Killing my wife?" He eyed her carefully. The way she flinched and the pain on her face had to be real or she was one hell of an actress.

"I swear to you I didn't kill Elizabeth." Soo wiped a tear off her cheek, her dark brown eyes filled with sadness and pain. "She was my mentor. I looked up to her and wanted to be just like her."

"Then why'd you do it?" He glanced around the empty, cold, stark room. The only person there was the guard in the corner standing watch. Mack lowered his voice, not knowing who he could trust anymore. "Why'd you steal the money?"

"I needed the money." A wave of shame swept over Soo's features. "I went to college on a gymnastics scholarship. I had a pretty bad accident and broke my neck. They put me on some pretty serious pain killers. It didn't take long for me to get addicted to them. I had a dealer in Massachusetts, but once I graduated and landed the job in the mayor's office, I didn't have anyone in town to help me out." Her eyes pleaded for understanding. "Addiction is a terrible thing, Mr. Buchanan. It can make a person desperate."

"Elizabeth would have helped you if you had told her, you know." Mack's voice filled with compassion. He and Elizabeth both had always had a soft spot for Soo. That's why her betrayal had hurt so much. "It took a lot for us to have a baby. I think that's why she loved kids and wanted to do everything she could for them. You were fresh out of college and an athlete. She would have helped you kick the addiction."

"I was too embarrassed and ashamed to tell her." Soo wiped away more tears and blew her nose. "I wanted her to think I was strong like her. Everyone knew how much she favored the youth program, so I figured they wouldn't realize if just a little more money went toward that program. I created a fake event that part of the money went to with no one the wiser until the Feds started poking around."

"But you didn't stop then, did you?"

"I kept telling myself I would stop. That I just needed one more fix, and then I would feel better, get stronger. She was all about helping kids, and I needed help in a big way. That was how I justified it." A sob slipped out, and her slight shoulders shook. "After she died, I was heartbroken. At that point I didn't care anymore. Zuckerman took over and kept me on, but the youth program was discontinued."

"How did you get the money for drugs after that?"

"I was terrified. I skimmed a little off all the programs I could, but it wasn't enough. I met Barry Granger at the bar, and he hit on me. I'd heard a few rumors around Zuckerman's office, so I propositioned Granger. I gave him what he wanted in exchange for him getting me a fix. Sheriff Pratt turned a blind eye in exchange for a cut of the money Barry got."

"How do Evans and Zuckerman figure into the equation?"

"Sheriff Evans and Mayor Zuckerman would do anything to gain power, and Pratt knew that, so he enlisted them into his schemes, promising them great rewards. He promised Evans the election as his successor, and he pulled some strings to make sure Zuckerman got all the political favors he needed." Disgust replaced sadness in Soo's eyes.

"A lot of things are starting to make sense now." Mack's jaw tightened.

"After Pratt retired down south, it was too late for either of the men to change, and by then I was in too deep. I kept their secrets, but they sure didn't think twice about selling me out. They've kept me locked up here to keep me quiet, threatening my family if I said anything. I honestly think if they hadn't been caught today, I never would have made it to trial. They would have found a way to get rid of me."

"That's not going to happen. You're safe now. Tell me one thing. Did Elizabeth know about any of this?"

"She was suspicious about something back then, especially after the Feds showed up and started asking her all sorts of questions. And then, when they asked about you and your crew, she started poking around on her own, but not because she thought you were guilty. She was determined not to let anyone ruin your name."

He smiled tenderly. "I've never questioned Beth's love for me. The same as I know she never questioned mine for her. What we had was special and rare. But I do know she would do anything to protect me. Do you think one of them could have killed her because of what she might have found out?"

Soo's face looked pensive before responding, "I think any of them are capable of something like that, but I'm not sure if they actually did it."

"You have been very helpful, Soo. I appreciate it. If you can think of anything, please give me a call." He opened his wallet and pulled out a piece of paper with his phone number written on it. The copy he'd made of the blackmail note fell onto the table.

Soo's eyebrows raised. "Wait, what's that?"

"You mean Sheriff Evans hasn't shown you this yet?"

"No, why?"

"It's the blackmail note they say you wrote after Elizabeth found out about you embezzling money from the program."

"I never wrote that note," she said with conviction and sincerity. "They told me she found out and I threatened to ruin her legacy, so we met in private and I killed her to keep her from talking. I haven't seen any evidence yet because I haven't had my trial, and like I said, they had no intention of turning me over to a jury."

"Do you know who could have written the note?"

"Other than the people we've already mentioned, no." Soo's eyes widened. "Except maybe someone who didn't like her platforms, or maybe...."

"What?"

"Well, Elizabeth was all about helping athletes go as far in life as they could by bringing in scouts and hosting events. But she was always fair. If you veered off the straight and narrow, you were out. Needless to say not all the parents were happy with her."

Mack had never thought to consider that angle. It made him remember something someone had said to him recently. "Thank you, Soo. You've helped more than you know." He got up and left, suddenly knowing exactly where he was going. And if he was right, he would kill the son-of-a-bitch himself.

177

17

IF YOU TELL what you know, so will I. We need to talk. If you don't want your career ruined, meet me at Mariner's Marina on the old, abandoned pier up the coast at sundown tonight. Tell no one where you're going, or there will be consequences.

TERROR GRIPPED my muscles and refused to let go as I held a copy of the same blackmail note Elizabeth Buchanan had received a decade ago in my shaking hands. The note that had changed all our lives forever. Gray storm clouds hovered above the cove, ready to burst open at any moment and unleash their wrath, matching my mood perfectly. This couldn't be happening. The case was closed. Last I'd heard Soo Young Lee was still in jail. I knew she wasn't the real killer, but they didn't.

Or did they?

Stacy Buchanan had messed with my life enough. I couldn't take it anymore. Constantly living in fear, waiting and wondering when the hammer was going to drop on everything I held dear. It was bullshit. One tiny little mistake years ago. An act of necessity to protect what was mine. Anyone would do the same if they had been faced with what I had been.

I shredded the note into tiny pieces and stuffed it into my pocket. It had been folded in half and placed under my windshield wiper, right out in the open. I had finished lunch at The Diner, watching the news clip about the crazy shit that had just gone down. The whole fucking town was falling apart.

All because of Stacy Buchanan.

I had spoken to a few people, making small talk, and then I'd headed outside. My stomach had dropped when I saw the note. At first I had thought it was a parking ticket, but when I opened it, I'd nearly had a heart attack. Anyone could have picked it up and read it. The game we were playing was getting deadly. Realization dawned.

They were trying to set me up.

I wasn't foolish enough to show up at Mariner's Marina just because they said so. And by they, I mean the Buchanans and the chosen ones who insisted on helping them. The police would surely be there, and I couldn't have that. I did agree, this charade had to stop, but I was the puppet master. I wasn't about to let them take control. A new sense of purpose filled me. Change of plans.

Sundown it would be...but I wouldn't be the one dying.

* * *

MACK SET everything in motion in preparation for sundown that night, and then he went home to make his final preparations there. He would miss his ray of sunshine lighting up his heart. But he couldn't bear to see the light leave her eyes when his mind went. And it would. There was no avoiding that. It was hell getting old. Mack was a man who liked being in control. When something was out of his control, he felt powerless.

All that was about to change.

Mack sat in his car at Mariner's Marina, waiting and watching as the sun set. The clouds had darkened to a slate gray, ominous and foreboding for what was to come. Even the wildlife and birds had taken shelter. He was ready. Prepared. His conscience clear. No one had shown up yet. Maybe his suspicion had been wrong, but his gut told him he was spot on.

Mack decided he would wait a while longer. Sitting there in silence, he thought about Stacy. She hadn't come home earlier. Here he'd finally convinced her to open up to Trent, but then the man had to go and ruin that. Mack was a good judge of character. He still thought Trent was a good man no matter whose last name he bore. Mack tried to tell her that, but his stubborn girl didn't listen to a word he had said this morning. After seeing the news report, she'd stormed out in a fury of rage.

Mack shook his head, thinking that poor boy didn't stand a chance.

Mack actually owed Trent and his old man a debt of gratitude. Special Agent Robert West had never been the bad guy in his eyes. He'd been the only one who didn't believe that Elizabeth had died by accident. He might have been guilty of dragging their name through the mud in trying to prove they were involved in illegal doings at first, but Mack knew he had only been doing his job.

West had backed off the second Elizabeth had died. If his son hadn't been so persistent in getting at the truth, the real culprits who'd done Mack's family wrong would still be free. Trent had not only gotten vindication; he'd erased any lingering tarnish about any aspect of the Buchanan name. Mack could live with that.

He just wasn't so sure Stacy could.

Speaking of Stacy, he called her cell but she didn't answer. That wasn't like her. She always answered her phone, especially when it was him. Glancing around the marina, there was still no sign of life. A chill swept through Mack as a deadly realization hit him. Something was wrong. The real killer wasn't going to show, and Mack suddenly knew why. Shit...

The killer was going after Stacy.

* * *

AFTER HOURS of feeling sorry for himself, he'd gone to see his dad. Trent took a chance and told him everything like he used to. It was as if the years had been erased and his father was his *dad* again. Trent decided to take his father's advice and not let the love of his life get away because of the job like his father had. Trent wasn't going to give up. Stacy meant too much to him to let her get away. He would convince her he loved her and she loved him and they needed to be together if it was the last thing he did.

But first he had to find her.

Stacy wasn't returning his calls. He'd checked in with her friend Laura, but she hadn't seen her. He knew Stacy was a private person. Other than Laura, she wouldn't confide in anyone except her father. He shifted uncomfortably in his car as he drove over to their house, knowing Mack would have his balls when he found out Trent had hurt his daughter. It wouldn't matter one bit that he'd never meant to and it had killed him to do so.

Pulling into their driveway, Trent parked around back like he used to. She'd said she never wanted to see him again. He prayed like hell she didn't mean it. Her car wasn't there and neither was Mack's. Trent climbed out of his truck, his boots crunching on the gravel. He glanced at the sky, stalling. It would be dark soon and stormy by the looks of it. He stood there a moment, gathering his nerve, and finally knocked. No one answered. Going on instinct, he tried the door and frowned. It was unlocked, even after all she had been through. He stepped inside to see if he could find a clue to where she might be.

His eyes were drawn immediately to the kitchen table. There was a note.

* * *

Dear Dad,

Sorry I missed your call earlier, but I wasn't in the mood for company. I'm still not. That's why I am writing this note instead of calling you back. I know if I talk to you, I will only start crying again. Louis Vito called and said he wanted to see me. I can't go there with puffy eyes and a red nose, but don't worry about me. I will catch up with you when I get home.

Love,
Your Little Mermaid

TRENT SET the note back down exactly where she had placed it. He felt like a real ass for making her upset. The last thing he ever wanted to do was hurt her. But sliding back into self-pity wouldn't solve anything. Words were cheap. He needed to show her how much she meant to him, starting right now.

Trent left Stacy's house and ten minutes later he pulled into the parking lot of Louis Vito's office. Being a cop, he couldn't help always scanning his surroundings. Once again, Stacy wasn't there. He climbed out of his truck and jogged up the steps to enter Louis' plush office. He spoke to the secretary, who disappeared into a room behind her for a moment, and then reappeared saying Louis was free. For Trent to go right in.

"Well, Mr. Clark...or should I say Special Agent West?" Louis' smile was pleasant enough as he walked around his desk to shake Trent's hand, but he had a calculating gleam in his eye. There was a reason the people in his circle called him the deadly teddy bear. He might look soft and cuddly, but those who underestimated him paid a deadly price in the courtroom. "What can I do for you, son?"

"I'm looking for Ms. Buchanan. She left a note saying she came to see you. I need to talk to her about some official business." Trent donned his most professional expression.

Louis chuckled. "You can't fool me, son. I know a man in love when I see it, but make no mistake..." Louis stared him down with hard eyes "...if you bring any more hurt to that family, I will bury you."

Trent held up his hands. "Fair enough."

"Smart man." Louis' face transformed back into a jovial teddy bear. "For the record, she could do worse." He winked.

"I appreciate that. Can I ask if you know where she went? It's really important that I speak to her."

"Well, I was going over some things her father wanted me to from his will, when she got a call saying her father found a better place to go to than Whispering Pines. Something about it being the perfect spot, and he wanted to show it to her. She wrote down the address, and off she went."

Just then Mack himself walked into the office with a look on his face that sent chills down Trent's spine. "Where is she?"

Trent and Louis shot each other a confused look and said simultaneously, "Supposedly with you."

"The hell she is," Mack bellowed and then clutched his heart.

"Mack, are you okay?" Trent grabbed the man's arm to steady him.

"I'm fine." The tough old man brushed off Trent's hand, too proud not to stand on his own for as long as he could.

"Look, about what happened this morning...I'm sorry."

Mack nodded once. "Good enough for me."

"You mean you're not mad?" Trent let out a rush of air he hadn't realized he'd been holding.

"Didn't say that." The old man gave Trent a look that made his throat go suddenly dry. Jesus the man could be intimidating, and Trent didn't intimidate easily.

"Roger that." Trent stood straight, prepared to take his punishment like a man. He deserved worse for deceiving them both. Mack's next words took him by surprise and gave him hope.

"You love my daughter. A blind man can see that. She's stubborn, but I know that she loves you too. You make her happy, and that's more important than you being a cop and lying to me about it. She's going to need someone like you when I'm gone."

"Don't say that, Mack. You don't know—"

"Yes, I do. My days are numbered, but I'm not worried about that. I'm worried about my daughter. I stopped home to find her note so I came here. Louis wasn't supposed to go over those documents until tomorrow." He nailed Louis with a hard glare. Louis held up his hands in an apologetic gesture. "We'll talk about that later. What did you mean when you said she was with me?"

Louis told Mack the same thing he had told Trent.

"We're too late." Mack's face paled. "He has her."

"Who?" Trent's eyebrows formed a deep V.

It took a minute, but Mack finally got out in a weak voice, "The real killer."

Fear like Trent had never known latched onto him. For a moment he couldn't breathe, but his cop instincts took over. He pulled himself together and gripped Mack's shoulders gently but firmly. "We're not going to lose her, Mack. Do you hear me?"

Mack's glazed eyes locked onto Trent's, and he struggled to focus. Finally, his expression cleared and he nodded.

"Good. Because I can't do this alone. I need your help. Think hard. Do you have any idea who the killer is? And where is Stacy? She said something about going to a better place. About finding the perfect spot. Do you know what she was talking about?"

Mack's eyes widened and Trent could tell the moment his words registered. The fog lifted from Mack and a sharpness like Trent had never seen crystalized in its place. He stepped out of Trent's hold, shot Louis a meaningful look, and headed for the door with long, purposeful strides.

"What is it?" Trent asked hot on his heels.

Mack paused long enough to look over his shoulder at Trent. Anger seeped out of his every pore, and Trent knew without a doubt he would murder the man for daring to harm his daughter if he had the chance.

"I know exactly where she is," Mack said and left without looking back.

18

STACY PULLED into a narrow driveway deep in the woods on the outskirts of town. She couldn't imagine her father wanting to live someplace like this. It was so far away from everything he enjoyed in town, but for his sake, she would at least take a look at it. She owed him that. Following the winding drive, she navigated her car up the hill until she broke through the trees into a clearing.

Her mouth fell open in awe. She hadn't expected this gem to appear out of nowhere. A gorgeous two story log cabin with a wall of windows sat facing a placid lake. The grounds were beautiful and spacious with hard and soft landscaping of stone and brick patios, shrubs, flowers, and mulch. Cozy furniture, tables, and a fire pit were artfully arranged to look so inviting. A sweeping lawn led out to the water. At the edge of the water, a long dock had a boat tied up to it, calmly waiting for the next fisherman to take her out.

Okay, she could see how this would appeal to her father. He'd been acting so strange lately. This would be just like him to want to go someplace peaceful where he could fish and live out his days without everyone he knew seeing him fade away until his mind was no longer there. He was too proud of a man to handle that. Knowing her father, he had probably taken care of everything. He would have enough money from the sale of the house to live however he wanted to. He could hire someone to take care of the house and grounds.

Louis had said her father had changed his will, specifying his wishes for everything: his money, his healthcare, his funeral, etc. Louis hadn't had a chance to give her all the details before she'd gotten a phone call, telling her of the better place her father had found. The perfect spot. Stacy had told him they would continue their conversation later. That she had to go before it got too dark out. She'd written down the address and left.

Now that she was here, she climbed out of her car and walked through the side yard, taking in everything up close as she made her way down to the water. It really was a beautiful place. Her mind was already thinking ahead. She meant what she said about sticking around and being there for her father. She wanted whatever time he had left to be happy. If this place made him happy, then that's all that mattered.

"It's beautiful, isn't it?" came a voice from behind her.

Stacy turned around with a smile on her face. "Hi, Gary, I'm glad you called. I didn't think I would make it before sunset."

"I'd say you're just in time." He had an odd look on his face. A half smile, but it somehow didn't look natural. "I've always loved a good sunset."

It was probably just her imagination. She shrugged off her uneasiness. "I have to admit, I was a little leery of Dad living way out here, but I can see why it's so special to him. If this is what he wants, then I think he should have it."

"I think you're making a smart decision." Gary stepped onto the dock and looked around the lake before meeting her eyes. "I think he should get exactly what he deserves."

"How much is the owner asking?" She turned back to study the house.

Stacy frowned. Wait a minute. From this angle, the house suddenly looked very familiar. That wall of windows...where had she seen that before? She swallowed hard as her uneasy feeling intensified, making the hairs on the nape of her neck stand up.

"Well, you see, that's the thing," Gary said from right beside her, making her jump back. He stepped in front of her, blocking her path off the dock. "I'm not so sure the current owner wants to sell. He's kind of attached to the place."

He...

Louis Vito!

This picture hung in his office. She had literally just been admiring it an hour ago. What on earth was happening? She was afraid she already knew the answer. Slowly walking back a couple steps, she held her ground and raised her chin a notch, trying for a bravado she didn't feel. The wind picked up, whirling around them, ruffling Gary's unkempt hair with a foreboding sense of doom.

"You're him, aren't you?" she breathed out in barely more than a whisper.

Those eyes. How had she not recognized them? Even with a ski mask on, she'd had a moment of staring into them when he was choking the life out of her. But then she'd been so focused on escaping, she'd forgotten the details until this very moment. He was still the same Gary Sanders she'd known forever. The father of her friend, Chase Sanders. The same man who had gone through a tragedy just like her family.

"You killed my mother." She was shaking her head in disbelief. "We trusted you. And you tried to kill me. How could you?"

"I didn't want to do it, if that helps." He actually looked sincere for a moment, like the man she remembered as a kid, yet a hint of crazy sparkled in his eyes. "But some things are unavoidable."

"Chase was my friend. He would have been so disappointed in you."

Gary's face hardened, changing him into the paranoid monster he had become. "Chase is the reason I'm in this mess." He took a step toward her while pulling on his gloves.

She backed up another step, thankful for the long pier, the wood creaking beneath her feet. "What are you talking about?" She had to keep him talking.

"None of this would have happened if it weren't for the steroids. Your mother found out and threatened to disqualify him from the event with all the scouts. Well, she didn't know my boy got his drugs from Barry, and Barry liked to talk when he drank. He let it slip about the mayor's office skimming money from the youth program."

"So you wrote the blackmail note to my mother?"

"I didn't write the note. Chase did. I didn't know anything about it, but I knew something was up with him. He was acting strange, so I followed him. I was shocked when I saw them arguing on the pier at Mariner's Marina. I spied on them and heard everything. Chase didn't mean her any harm. He was trying to get her to keep quiet about him, and in return he would keep quiet about her office. She said she didn't know anything about that, but she would look into it. But that didn't mean she would allow him to get away with cheating. She said if he dropped out and came clean, then she would help him."

So that's how Chase was better than everyone else. He was talented already. He could have gone so far, yet he'd taken the easy way out. Or he'd done it to please his father who had always put so much pressure on him to be his meal ticket out of debt.

"I don't understand." She tried to think of anything to keep him talking. "Why would you kill her if she was going to help your son?"

"I didn't have a choice. Chase flew into a rage from the drugs. He started choking her, and she collapsed to the ground. Just as quickly, he freaked out over what he had done. I thought he was going to kill himself when he saw me. I told him to go home and not say a word, and I would take care of it. I thought she was already dead, so I was just burying her. When I realized she was alive, I knew I couldn't let her live."

Gary wasn't even looking at Stacy, he was rambling like a maniac in his own world as if trying to justify to himself why he'd done it. She was inching her way around him. Just a little more space and she could make a run for her car. Too late. He met her eyes and moved to fill the space.

"Your mother would have ruined Chase. She brought it on herself. My boy was special. He was going places, gonna be a big star, and she tried to take all that away." The look on his face made it clear he actually believed what he was saying. "I couldn't let him miss his chance with the scouts."

"You're a monster." Stacy shook with anger, overriding her fear. How dare he stand before her and try to justify what he'd done?

Gary's face darkened and he clenched his hands into fists. "I had nothing! My wife left me. I lost all my money from gambling. Chase was all I had left." He swiped his hands through the air. "I wasn't about to let your mother take him away from me too, dammit."

"Instead you took my mother away from me and my father!" she shouted back, unable to help herself. "How is that fair? We never did anything to you. Chase wasn't special," she sneered, wanting to hurt him like he had her. "His scholarship was a lie. I heard he was high as a kite when he died in that car crash. You ruined him by making him live with this. And in the end you lost him to drugs anyway, so all of this was for nothing."

"It wasn't for nothing. His reputation is still intact, and I intend to keep it that way. I worked hard to re-build my life in this town. I'm respected. I won't let you take what I have left away from me. You're meddle-some just like your mother." Gary's tone grew to an eerie calm. "If you had just left well enough alone, none of this would be necessary."

She looked around, her eyes darting everywhere as she desperately tried to think of a way out as she con-tinued to stall. "You picked Louis' house to frame him, didn't you?"

"I didn't cover my tracks well enough last time. I'm not about to make that mistake again." It started to rain in big fat drops. "Enough with all the talking." He started walking toward her with his gloved hands out in front of him. "It's time."

She backed up, knowing she didn't have anywhere else to go. "You won't get away with this. Someone will find me."

"No they won't. No one lives here, and by the time Louis' divorce is finalized, you'll be nothing but bones at the bottom of this lake." He lunged for her.

Stacy didn't hesitate. She reacted on instinct, twisting away, his fingers brushing her shirt but failing to latch on as she pushed off the dock with her legs. Her body lunged into a perfect arc as she dove into the water behind her, barely making a ripple. The water closed over her in a welcome, familiar embrace.

Breaking the surface, she swam with long, sure strokes away from the shore.

The rain came down harder now. Thunder boomed and lightning streaked across the darkening sky. Terrified he was right behind her, she stopped swimming and started treading water as she turned around and faced the shore.

"You can't stay out there forever," Gary yelled from the end of the dock.

She breathed a sigh of relief, refusing to respond.

He hadn't followed her, pacing back and forth like he didn't quite know what to do. He must not be a strong swimmer she realized, but he was right. Even she had her limits. The water was cold, and her clothes felt like weights. She couldn't help but think of her mother at this moment, sinking to her death from the weight of an anchor pulling her down.

The rain was pouring now, and Stacy began to shiver. She didn't know how much time had gone by, but she began to tire. She kicked her shoes off, and then stripped off her pants and shirt, letting them sink to the bottom of the lake. She wasn't in the same shape she had been in her college days. Left in nothing but her bra and panties, she floated on her back for a while until she heard the sound of an engine. Lifting her head, she looked toward the shore but didn't see Gary.

She didn't see the boat anymore either.

Hearing the motor get closer, she looked to the side and saw it coming straight at her. There was no way she could outswim the boat. He was going to run her over. She took a big breath and dove deep, swimming down as fast as she could. She felt the water surge past her as the boat buzzed right over her, just missing her by her feet. Quickly swimming back up to the surface, she broke through the water and gasped for breath.

Gary had turned the boat around and was headed

her way once more. Stacy was exhausted, but her will to live spurred her into motion. Inhaling a deep breath, she dove beneath the surface and swam hard again, deeper this time. The bottom of the boat hit her foot, the engine coming within inches of slicing her open. Her body spun as if she were in the drum of a clothes dryer, tossing her about and disorienting her. When she stopped spinning, her foot became entangled in the tall seaweed. A moment of panic bubbled up inside her, threatening to consume her.

Stacy started kicking frantically, only making things worse, but then a calmness surrounded her as a voice in her head urged her to relax. Panic was not her friend. She must remember her training. Stacy blinked, looking around the dark water for an explanation, but she didn't see anything. Yet she was absolutely certain her mother was with her. Stacy suddenly understood that no matter where she went or what she chose to do, her mother would always be with her. That brought her a source of comfort.

Closing her eyes, Stacy concentrated. She bent over and focused on her ankle, saving her energy for when she would need it. It only took a moment to untangle the seaweed from around her foot. Using as much energy as she had left, she kicked toward what was left of the daylight. It felt like forever, but finally she broke the surface and with that came the cold hard truth.

She wasn't going to make it.

She couldn't keep going at this pace, she thought as she sucked in gulp after gulp of air. All she could think about was Trent. She'd been so hurt, she'd let her stubbornness and pride get in the way. His father meant the world to him, just like hers did to her. Of course he would have done anything to help him, just as she would. So what if Trent was a cop. She knew the type of man he was, and they didn't get any better than that.

Throwing away what they had over her insecurities was dumb.

Now she would die without ever getting to tell him she loved him, too.

An engine sounded once more, and she knew if she went under again, she wouldn't have the strength to make it back to the top. Her tears mixed with rain as they streamed down her face. She turned to the side and saw the boat headed her way once more. Accepting her fate, she waited for the inevitable.

Suddenly the boat slowed down and circled around her, coming to a stop. This was it. Stacy's heart pounded as she looked up and saw a pair of eyes staring down at her, but they didn't belong to Gary. Trent reached out a hand, and Stacy let out a sob. He'd come for her. She held out her hand, and he grabbed her wrist, pulling her up over the edge. He started to back away, but she threw herself into his arms.

"I'm so sorry," he said, wrapping her in a fierce hug.

"I know. Me too." She kissed him hard and then leaned back to look deep into his beautiful eyes. "I love you, too, Trent Clark West, whoever you are."

His gaze widened in surprise. "You do?" He cupped her face, looking like he wasn't quite believing what was happening. "I thought I'd ruined everything." He swallowed hard, moisture filling his hazel eyes. "I thought I'd lost you for good."

She nodded and started to cry. "I-I was so afraid I wasn't going to get to tell you before I died."

He hugged her to him hard, letting her know how he felt with every ounce of his flesh. "Shhh, it's okay, baby. I've got you now, and I'm never letting you go. I love you so damn much."

She buried her face in his chest, and he held her tight but didn't say a word until she stopped shivering and her tears subsided. Then he guided her to the wheelhouse to join her father, wrapping her in a towel and keeping her close, leaving Gary in an unconscious heap out in the rain, chained to the railing with handcuffs. She met her father's loving gaze, thinking he looked so perfect behind the wheel of a boat. Big and strong and larger than life.

Her captain of the seas.

It used to be his arms she ran to when she was scared or needed help, but something about being in Trent's arms now felt so right. Her father nodded to her once, as if reading her thoughts again with acceptance and approval. She knew he was relieved she had someone to lean on because as much as she hated to admit it, he was right. He wouldn't be around forever, and she really didn't want to go through life alone, no matter how much she had said so.

Stacy kept her arms around Trent, needing his warmth and strength. "How did you find me?"

"Your father remembered Louis saying his cabin was a better place and Gary being able to find the perfect spot for anything," Trent explained. "He'd found the perfect spot to hide your mother's body, and your father's gut was telling him he'd found the perfect spot to dispose of you. It was a longshot. I'm just glad it payed off. When we got here, we saw what was happening out on the lake. Louis had a jet ski. I'm just glad we got to Gary in time to stop him. Your father's one hell of a captain."

Her father's gaze met Trent's with affection and respect as he responded, "And you're one hell of a cop, son."

A calmness settled over Stacy. For the first time in a long time, she felt at peace. She felt happy. Justice would be served, and maybe she really could have it all.

EPILOGUE

MACK WALKED UP HIS DRIVEWAY, exhausted. They'd caught Elizabeth's killer, and Gary was going away for a very long time. To think his old friend had murdered his wife. Mack knew all about doing anything for family, but Gary hadn't saved his son at all by ignoring a drug problem he'd pushed him into in the first place out of his obsession for his son to be the best. He'd lost him in the end anyway, and had created a life that was a lie.

But all that was over now.

Stacy had found Trent and they were happy. The FBI had lifted Bob West's ban on being in the Cove, so he had returned to his normal looking self, surprising quite a few. Roy had agreed to keep him on since he made a decent stern man, and Bob was enjoying feeling useful again while getting reacquainted with his son. Barry Granger was locked up where he deserved to be, as well as Sheriff Pratt, Sheriff Evans, and Thomas Zuckerman, who were doing time for their crimes. Soo Young Lee was getting help while she served her time, and then she would get out and go on to be the person Elizabeth had believed in.

Everything was set in his world now. It was time to

finish what he'd started. He had to admit he was scared, but he couldn't bear to have the people he loved the most going through any more pain. It was the least he could do for them. His one final act of heroism. He just hadn't expected to feel this sadness. He wasn't really ready for this crazy ride to be over with, but he felt helpless and alone. Hiding his pain like he always did, he opened the door and walked inside the house that had been his home for the better part of his life.

"Have a seat, Dad," Stacy said as she sat down at their kitchen table. "It's time for a family meeting."

He looked at Trent on one side of Stacy and Olivia on the other. A corner of his lip tipped up ever so slightly, but he didn't say a word of denial. He knew she was right. These people were his family. So he sat and said, "What is this, an intervention?"

"So to speak," Olivia said in total doctor mode now. "Do you have a problem with that, Mr. Buchanan?"

"Not at all. You've all got something on your mind, so spill it."

"You're not a quitter, Dad. Suicide is not the answer." Stacy's beautiful amber eyes filled with concern and fear and sadness. Everything he'd wanted to avoid.

He blinked, surprised she had figured out his plan to sail off into the sunset and sink his boat. The ocean was by far a better place than losing his mind. It was the best thing for all of them. They would see that eventually.

"I have to follow protocol and take you in for observation for twenty-four hours, but I sure as hell am not about to let you take the coward's way out, you old stubborn mule." Olivia was back, and her sea-foam green eyes froze him with icicles. "Modern medicine has come a long way. You could live for years before losing your memories. Let me help take care of you. You don't have to be alone. You are *not* a coward,

Mackenzie Buchanan. You are the most amazing man I've ever known. I know you don't love me like I do you, but I love you enough for the both of us. And I can tell you that Elizabeth would approve, so quit being afraid and denying me the years you have left."

They were all a bit surprised by her words, but no one said anything.

"I'm not selling the house," Stacy said. "I'm not afraid anymore. Coldwater Cove feels like home again. I'm going to live here with you. And before you say what about my career, let me tell you what I really want to do. Swimming has always been my first love. I'm going to take over coaching the swim team at the local high school. I've already talked to the school board, and they're in agreement. And the paper has offered me a job in the sports section. You see? I'll be getting the best of both worlds. With my connections, I can do so much for the teens. Laura is going to run for mayor. She would be perfect, and the town loves her. Together we can bring back Mom's youth program."

"I'm staying too, Mack. Let's just say I have a couple of big reason for wanting to stick around." Trent winked at Stacy, then returned a sincere, honest gaze back to Mack. "I only joined the FBI to help my dad. I've done that. I'm tired of moving and ready to settle down. I'm thinking I might run for sheriff. I have some connections that can pull some strings for me. I think it's time the sheriff's department and the mayor's office worked in sync for once. It's time we made the Cove the great place it once was." His eyes softened. "The place your wife had dreamed it could be again."

"So what do you say, Dad?"

Mack studied each of them, finding it hard to speak. Here he'd thought he'd be a burden to them. He hadn't wanted to cause any of them more pain, but he'd come to realize his leaving this world early would have cheated them of time with him. Time was a precious thing, no matter how special or painful. He would hang on to what moments he had left with the ones he loved, and not look back. Suddenly the sadness and fear that had weighed him down for so long now lifted. He wasn't alone. He was loved.

He felt exhilarated and alive for the first time in a long time.

"I say I love you." Mack reached his hand out and squeezed Stacy's, then nodded to Trent.

Trent put his arm around Stacy who smiled, her eyes filling with happiness.

Turning to Olivia, Mack took both her hands in his own. He met her eyes with all the love he felt for her, realizing it was true and that was okay. He didn't have to feel guilty. Olivia was right. Elizabeth would have wanted this.

"I love *all* of you," he said softly.

She blinked back tears and smiled, holding on tight.

"So I say yes. Let's do this thing." Mack laughed, feeling lighter than he had in years. As if Elizabeth had given her blessing, the sun came out...

And suddenly the dark seas of Coldwater Cove weren't so dark anymore.

To everyone! The past two years have been hard. Never did I think the whole world would live through a pandemic. As we start to turn a corner for the better, I hope we become stronger, kinder, and more mindful about the world, ourselves, and each other. Here's to hoping the seas in 2022 are a little less dark. Much love, health, and happiness to you all 😌

ABOUT THE AUTHOR

Kari Lee Townsend is a National Bestselling Author of mysteries & a tween superhero series. She also writes romance and women's fiction as Kari Lee Harmon. With a background in English education, she's now a full-time writer, wife to her own superhero, mom of 3 sons, 1 darling diva, 1 daughter-in-law & 2 lovable fur babies. These days you'll find her walking her dogs or hard at work on her next story, living a blessed life.

ALSO BY THE AUTHOR

WRITING AS KARI LEE HARMON
Destiny Wears Spurs
Spurred by Fate
Project Produce
Love Lessons
Until Tomorrow
Valley of Secrets

Coldwater Cove
Dark Seas

COMFORT CLUB SERIES
Sleeping in the Middle

MERRY SCROOGE-MAS SERIES
Naughty or Nice
Sleigh Bells Ring
Jingle All The Way

LAKE HOUSE TREASURES SERIES
The Beginning
Amber
Meghan
Brook

WRITING AS KARI LEE TOWNSEND
A Kalli Ballas Mystery
Mind over Murder

Two Cents of Doom